P9-CEI-953

SAINT PHILOMENE'S INFIRMARY *for* MAGICAL CREATURES

W. STONE COTTER

SAINT PHILOMENE'S INFIRMARY *for* MAGICAL CREATURES

GODWIN BOOKS
HENRY HOLT AND COMPANY
NEW YORK

Henry Holt and Company, *Publishers since 1866*
Henry Holt® is a registered trademark of Macmillan Publishing Group, LLC
175 Fifth Avenue, New York, NY 10010
mackids.com

Library of Congress Control Number: 2017945047
ISBN 978-1-62779-257-8 (hardcover)
ISBN 978-1-62779-258-5 (ebook)

First edition, 2018 / Designed by April Ward
Printed in the United States of America by LSC Communications, Harrisonburg, Virginia

1 3 5 7 9 10 8 6 4 2

This book is dedicated to my
brilliant, shatterproof nephews,
Bobby, Jack Henry, William,
and Benjamin

And to my prodigiously talented
and insightful beta reader,
Claire Lily Greenberg

CHAPTER 1

On an unnaturally hot spring afternoon, the day after the last day of seventh grade, Chance Bee Jeopard, a brown-haired boy of narrow build whose ears stuck out perhaps a bit too far, was digging a hole in the backyard of the small house he shared with his older sister, Pauline, and their mother, Daisy, when *plork!* Chance's rusty old shovel hit something that was most certainly not dirt.

Chance was, before anything and above all, a tester of limits. He was a questioner of assertions, a taker of risks. Chance felt compelled to do things like hurl homemade javelins and overinflate basketballs and break ceiling tiles with his forehead and try to hold his breath longer than his friend at school Jiro Kurosawa (eighty-one seconds being the record to beat); in other words, Chance liked to do anything that dirtied his hands, challenged his body, or dared his mind.

Hole digging, it so happened, encompassed all of this. He wondered why he hadn't thought of it sooner.

Chance had been working on digging his hole every day after school for the last week, lifting shovelfuls of cool, loamy dirt from the deepening hole in the farthest corner of the backyard. There, he was conveniently shielded from his house by the crumpled tree house a twister had some years before knocked off its perch in the branches of a spreading pecan tree, the same tree that now provided Chance with a measure of relief from the sun as he dug, dug, dug.

It was to be the deepest hole in the small town of Starling, a place that held the distinction of being the hottest spot in all of Texas, which was saying quite a bit. Chance had borrowed a shovel from the next-door neighbor Mrs. Applebaker, whom Chance knew from experience was good with secrets.

The hole, currently seven and a half feet—two and a half feet deeper than Chance was tall—was deep enough that Chance could no longer heave dirt out of the hole with the shovel and was instead forced to haul it up a painter's ladder in a tin bucket. The hole was narrower at the bottom than the top, so Chance's work focused on widening as well as deepening it.

It was when Chance was thinking he'd like to dig six

more inches before he quit for the day that he suddenly struck something with his shovel. Something that felt like a . . . a *skull*. Or at least it sounded like what Chance imagined a skull poked with a shovel might sound like—a hollow, chalky *plork*. Whatever it was, he had broken it, leaving a small hole from which a quiet but continuous sucking sound emitted. It reminded Chance of the *fwussssh* of a can of tennis balls freshly opened.

Chance fought a moment of panic. What if there was a whole *body* down there, dead by some nefarious hand, its wakeful and disruptive ghost ready to haunt Chance now that he had violated its rest? Chance gripped the ladder and was about to start climbing as fast as he could when his senses returned. Ghosts didn't exist. There weren't demons or vampires or fairies or shellycoats or Querquetulanae or any of that stuff. At least that's what Pauline, his older sister, would have said, and Chance, as much as his sister bugged him, had to admit she was right, at least some of the time. Maybe most of the time. Okay, *all* the time.

So Chance closed his eyes, took two long breaths, innnn . . . ouuut . . . innnn . . . ouuut—his mother was an Ashtanga yoga instructor and expert breather, and she had taught her children well—then got down on his hands and knees to examine his discovery.

It wasn't a skull. It was a big pipe of some kind, made from the same sort of ceramic that flowerpots were made of. Judging by the curvature of the exposed bit, Chance estimated the pipe to be about two feet in diameter. He had caused a jagged, roundish hole with the tip of the shovel, large enough to get his hand through. The walls of the pipe looked like they were about an inch thick. He did not actually put his hand inside; he wasn't up for that kind of test today. What if there was hydrochloric acid in there? Or giant rabid rats? Or something no human had ever seen before—something with big, knifelike teeth as sharp as ocular scalpels and a slobbering appetite for human flesh?

So he kept his hands to himself. Nothing was leaking out of the pipe. There was only the sucking sound, which he realized was just rushing air; the pipe appeared to be a kind of wind tunnel. He carefully bent down and peered inside.

Nothing. Dark as the intergalactic medium.

Wait, what was that? Chance thought he saw something, a faint, dull-gray something, moving quickly. It was there, then it was gone.

Then, Chance heard something all too familiar in the late Texas spring: thunder. If there was ever an enemy of the seven-and-a-half-foot-deep backyard hole, it was a violent afternoon thunderstorm.

Chance riffled through his pockets, looking for something to jam in the hole he'd made in the pipe, but could find nothing. A fat ball of rain popped on the crown of his head. Another rolled down his back. A third exploded on the toe of his right sneaker.

Ah, of course. Chance kicked off his shoes. Then he

stripped off his socks, rolled them up, and stuck the sock balls in the hole. Better than nothing. The rain began to fall harder, like it meant business. Chance quickly climbed out and bolted for the house.

He ran inside, where he found that crimson-haired, hazel-eyed human curiosity, Pauline. She was sitting at the dining room table, studying something on a laptop. Pauline seemed to have grown six inches in the last month, her lanky form bent over the keyboard like a sapling in the wind. She looked up and stared intently at her brother.

Chance often wondered if Pauline knew whenever he was doing something he ought not be doing, like puncturing their property with big holes. Chance became conscious of the dirt covering his clothes. But he was usually covered in dirt. Pauline just rolled her eyes and returned to her computing.

As anyone within a hundred miles could have told you, Pauline Dearie Jeopard, freshly graduated from ninth grade, was, first and foremost, a *skeptic*. She was particularly skeptical of anything supernatural—werewolves, limbo, little green men, spontaneous human combustion, demonic possession, zombiism, underground realms, poltergeists and ghostly cold spots, psychic spoon bending, and telepathy. Especially telepathy.

No, Pauline believed in the empirical sciences, laboratories, the timeline of geology, the physics of space-time. The only magic in Pauline's life was the miraculous precision and flexibility of mathematics.

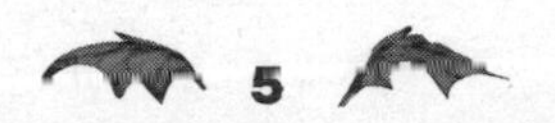

And the internet.

Pauline, excited about the coming thunderstorm, was searching the internet for photographs of fulgurites, as the subterranean tubal branches of fused minerals caused by lightning ground strikes were called, an example of which Pauline desperately wanted to find *in situ*—she did not want to buy one from a rock shop—when she looked up again to regard her dirt-covered little brother, who seemed a bit more dirt-covered than usual.

"Some people have an outdoor cat," said Pauline. "I have an outdoor brother. What have you been doing?"

"Nothing, nope, what have you been doing?"

"Research. Mom is not going to like all the extra dirt you brought in."

"I know, but it's starting to rain."

"I'm about to go out to the top of the Indian burial mound."

"But . . . lightning!"

"That's the reason I'm going out there," she said. Her eyes grew large. "You can see for *miles*."

"But . . . but . . . lightning will kill you," said Chance, waving his arms about, sprinkling dirt like cracked pepper on the floor. "You know that!"

"I'm going to wear rubber galoshes," said Pauline. "Plus, I'm going to lie down in the grass. Want to come?"

"No way, José. I don't want to get struck and killed by lightning. I have too many projects to finish."

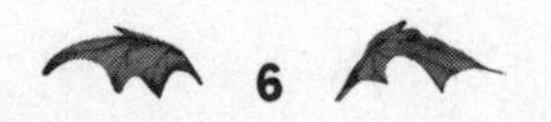

"Don't tell Mom," she said to her brother, sotto voce. Their mother, Daisy Bopp Jeopard, was in her room concentrating on *trikonasana*, one of the most strenuous and difficult positions in yoga. The day after tomorrow, she was heading to Denver to teach other instructors the niceties of Ashtanga Vinyasa yoga, a modern-day variant of the ancient discipline.

"I'm gonna."

"If you do, I'll tell her you've been digging a giant hole in the backyard."

Chance's eyes turned to perfect circles and his mouth dropped to the floor like an anvil.

Pauline left him there, then put on her raincoat and galoshes and slipped out the front door.

She pulled a shovel out of the dirt in her mother's garden of Knock Out roses, got on her red ten-speed, and pedaled as fast as she could out to the old Indian burial mound, a monolith of dirt a hundred feet in length rising forty feet above the surrounding terrain.

The storm was at full strength. The winds whipped up the flaps of her coat, the bullets of rain struck her body, the slaps of thunder deafened her. She finally reached the top of the ancient, muddied hill, tossed the shovel a safe distance away, lay flat on her stomach, and watched the horizon.

There! A lightning strike to a magnolia tree, more than a quarter of a mile away. And *whoa!* A strike to the lightning rod at the Barrows' ranch a few hundred yards to the north.

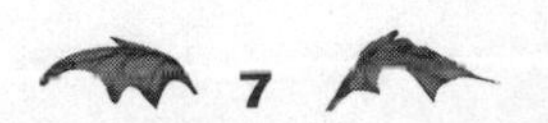

And *yow!* A bolt to an old Volkswagen bus bumbling down US Highway 123. The strike didn't even cause a hiccup in the vehicle's merry travels.

Strike after blinding strike erupted from the thundercloud above, but none hit the ground.

She squinted into the distance, waiting, waiting, as the horizontal rain battered her side.

Pauline wished Chance was with her. But she knew why he wasn't.

Dad.

Nothing had ever tested Chance, or Pauline, as severely as the events of an otherwise ordinary Tuesday less than one year before. They were thirteen and eleven then, and their moody, impenetrable second cousin, twenty-year-old Pye McAllister, was staying with them while Pauline and Chance's parents were out of town. Their mom was in Rhinebeck, New York, teaching Ashtanga Vinyasa yoga at the Omega Institute, and their dad, Albert Wuthering Jeopard (TV meteorologist *extraordinaire)*, was visiting central Florida, home of the most frequent and powerful lightning strikes on the planet, to partly fulfill his dream of experiencing the world's worst weather firsthand. He had endured the scorch of the Sahara and Death Valley; felt the lethal winds of Mount Washington in New Hampshire; suffered the cold at East Antarctic Plateau in the dead of winter—August—where in

2010 the world's coldest-ever temperature, –136°F, had been recorded. Central Florida was one of the few megaweather locales he had put off visiting, as he had more than just passing anxiety when it came to lightning; he suffered from full-fledged astraphobia. To overcome this, a trip to the lightning fields of Florida was requisite.

And there, near the town of Kathleen, on a low rise in a field much like the one Pauline was currently inhabiting, a serrate bolt tinted baby blue found Albert Jeopard, taking him instantly and painlessly out of this life.

CHAPTER 2

Chance stared out the sliding glass door at the sky. His sister had gone into the storm more than an hour before. More and more quickly, the crashes of thunder followed the lightning strikes that created them. The wind drove the raindrops into the door like rounds from a Gatling gun.

He knew he should go out there. But as much as he liked to test himself, take dares, push limits, *strive*, lightning was a different matter. It had intimidated even Dad, a man who'd once spent a spring chasing tornadoes, catching six. But Chance didn't want to get struck. He leaned his forehead against the glass, feeling the vibrations of the pelletlike rain strafing the other side. He prayed his sister would come back soon. Or that the storm would end. He didn't even care about his hole in the yard; he didn't care about the mysterious sucking pipe he'd breached; he didn't care if Mom caught him shedding dirt all over the dining room floor. He wanted his sister to come back.

He called his friend Jiro.

"'Sup," said Jiro.

"Nothing."

Chance wanted to mention that his sister was out in the storm by herself, and, somehow, he wanted Jiro to tell him it was okay that he hadn't gone out there with her.

"Wanna spend the night over here tomorrow night?" said Jiro.

A whisper of excitement stirred within Chance. It was fun at Jiro's house. He had triple bunk beds, a backyard with a stream running through it, a pellet gun, and a dad who told pretty funny jokes. And . . . Jiro had the internet. The real internet, not the dumb, restricted, hamstrung version he had at home.

"Yeah."

"'K, bye."

"'K, bye."

The wind began to die down. Thunder didn't crack so much as it rumbled, the edges of its sound rounded by distance. Before long, the sun was out, hot, and the world began to steam.

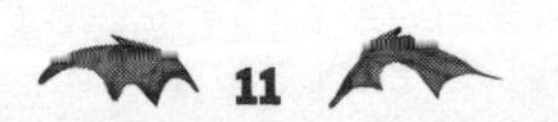

Just then a freight train went by. The alley behind the Jeopards' house ran parallel to a MoPac spur, and twice a day, a good long train went by.

Twice a year, the FanTan & Carlinda Circus train went by, half a mile long, painted in reds and greens and golds and bearing elephants and giraffes and lions in cages, the coaches moving barely fifteen miles an hour. The whole town gathered to watch it. The Jeopards assembled on the second floor of their house to view the spectacle.

The train was due to pass through town again in just a few days. Chance couldn't wait.

"Chance?" said his mother, emerging from her room. "Where's your sister? Oh, look at you. Worse than ever."

"Can I sleep at Jiro's tomorrow night?"

"Well . . ."

"Pleeeeeee—"

"Okay. But bathtub, now. Tiptoe. Don't touch anything but soap."

Daisy looked around for her daughter. She figured she was probably at her friend Mersey Marsh's, doing something obscure. Mersey was older than Pauline, and in certain ways more mature, in others less. She always dressed in black, her pretty face made up with a modestly Goth palette, and she occasionally augmented her look with two authentic-looking fangs that fitted perfectly onto her upper canines. Daisy was not sure if Mersey Marsh was the best influence. But the durability of their friendship surprised

Daisy. Mersey was all about the dark arts, psychic phenomena, supernatural beings, tarot, and related malarkey—all the things Pauline scoffed at. Yet they laughed and whispered and plotted and palled around like sorority sisters.

Daisy opened the front door from within at the same instant her daughter did from without.

"Mom, look what I have."

Pauline was holding something that looked like a twisted, melted candelabra encrusted with sand, or a mineralized antler bigger than her head.

"What—"

"A fulgurite. I found one. It's still hot—feel."

Daisy reached out to touch it. It was about as warm as the handle of a just-boiled teapot. She drew back her hand.

"Ow. Doesn't that hurt to hold?"

"Oh no."

"Where in the world did you get it?"

"Out of the ground, right where a bolt of lightning struck. I dug it up with your gardening thing. Where's Chance? I want to show him."

Chance happened to be in the tub, trying to clean under his fingernails with a bobby pin. Even though he knew he would be out in the yard slinging mud in a matter of minutes and some of that mud was destined for his fingernails, he worked at scrubbing his nails anyway to please his mother, who really liked her children to be clean.

A banging at the bathroom door.

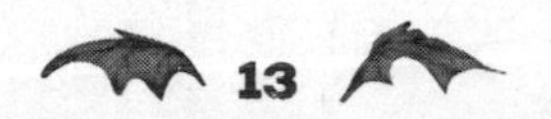

"Hurry up," said Pauline from the other side. "I have to show you something."

It wasn't until then that Chance realized how tense, how physically wound up, he'd been while his sister was out in the storm, because at the sound of her voice his body suddenly wholly relaxed, even his neck, which was holding up his as yet unshampooed head.

"Out soon," he said.

"Mersey is coming over, too. I know how much you like her."

Even though he was flushed red from the hot water, Chance could feel himself blush a shade or two darker. He simply could *not* make sense of the curious, fluttery feelings that swept through his body at the mention of his sister's strange friend Mersey Marsh.

"No, I don't, she's weird," said Chance, his voice coming out a bit squeakier than he meant it to. His sister just laughed.

Shampoo, rinse, repeat. Chance dried off and darted to his room. It was kind of silly of him to bathe and then head right out again to get filthy, but he'd had two baths many times. It was the lot of a tester of limits such as himself.

He dressed in a T-shirt and jeans and sneaked out to his backyard project, praying the mud wasn't too thick.

But it was. Chance sighed, then climbed down into his deepening hole. It took hours to get the mud out. By the time

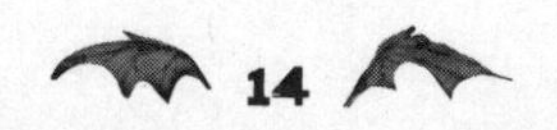

he finished, the sun was going down. The fireflies were out, carving greenish arcs in the darkening sky above him.

The socks he'd used to plug up the hole in the pipe were now a black snowball, utterly unwearable, but they had done their job. He tossed them aside, then got down on his hands and knees to investigate the hole. The brisk wind still whistled through the pipe, but it seemed otherwise empty. He found a stick and jammed it deep inside.

The stick jumped around in his hand; the wind inside blew with vigor.

Then, something *hit* the stick. *What in the world?* He peered into the pipe. Nothing but blackness.

Wait! A dim flash of light, gone as quickly as it had appeared, just like before. He put his ear to the hole. Over the wind, he could hear a very distant groan. It sounded a little like Chewbacca howling underwater.

Chance sat back, leaning against one wall of his muddy hole, as two voices in his head argued back and forth. *Should I?* No way, José! *You should because Dad would do it.* There's no way I'm putting anything else in there. *Why don't you do it to honor your dad?* Nuh-uh! *Do it.* No. *What's the worst that can happen?* Some knife-toothed monster will flay the skin off my arm, that's what. *That won't happen; your sister could tell you that.* Well, maybe. *Then do it.*

So Chance slowly worked his left hand into the pipe. Farther, farther, until he was up to his elbow. He couldn't feel the other side of the pipe; his hand just hung there in midair. It felt like he was sticking his arm out of a car going sixty miles per hour.

Suddenly, something hit his hand—*paper?*—not too hard, and then was gone. It took every nanogram of fortitude he had not to squeal, yank his arm out, climb out of the hole, and shovel all the dirt back in again as fast as he could.

But Chance knew himself pretty well. If he did that, he'd always wonder what was in this stupid pipe. Eventually, he would just dig it up again.

So Chance left his arm in the hole. For nearly ten minutes nothing happened, except that his arm grew chilled from the wind.

Then something wrapped itself around his wrist. Chance shrieked like a startled raccoon. It felt like a piece of ever-so-slightly damp paper. It stayed there, held in place by the wind.

He eased his hand out of the hole, the paper sliding farther and farther down his wrist, eventually winding up in his hand. He grasped it tight. Careful not to tear the paper on the jagged edges of the broken pipe, he drew it out.

It was a letter.

CHAPTER 3

There was a noise at the front door: *tikki-tik-tik-tik.* It was Mersey Marsh, who liked to "knock" by tapping her long midnight fingernails against the stained-glass pane in the door. Pauline let her in.

"You have to see this," Pauline said, leading her friend upstairs.

The ceiling of Pauline's room was dotted with hundreds and hundreds of little glow-in-the-dark stars. Just a foot below them, hanging by numerous lengths of fishing line, was a working antique orrery, the bronze ball representing the sun rotating ever so slowly as its glass-and copper planets and their moons revolved around it. And scattered about on Pauline's floor was pretty much her entire wardrobe, all among cardboard boxes filled with . . . stuff: broken microscopes, unfinished model F-15s, Legos and Lite-Brite pegs, collapsible fishing poles, broken slides for the broken microscopes, tons of agates and pieces of mica and flint and meteorites. The mess didn't faze Mersey Marsh; her room was worse.

Pauline opened one of the many boxes, pulled out her marvelous fulgurite, and handed it to her friend.

"What . . . what *is* this? It's beautiful."

Pauline explained fulgurites and detailed her trip into the storm to find one.

"So light," said Mersey. She studied it closely, sniffed it, then closed her eyes and put it up to her ear.

"Not even a pound," said Pauline, "according to the bathroom scale."

"This," said Mersey, "is a powerful object."

"What do you mean?"

"I swear it's vibrating. I think it can do . . . *things*."

"That's bananas," said Pauline, taking her fulgurite back. "It's just a rock—"

"I wonder if it's a conduit to another place," Mersey said, almost dreamily, clasping her hands together and looking up at the magnificent orrery. "Or another *time*. Or maybe it's a channel to the restless dead."

"That's all baloney, Mersey Marsh, and you know it."

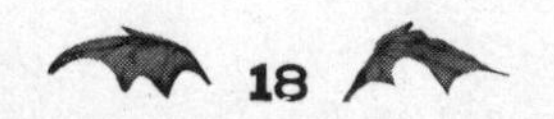

"Not."

Fourteen-year-olds were too old to say *not*, but oh how Pauline wanted to. Sometimes Mersey drove her up the wall.

"Let's go downstairs and make macaroni and cheese and say hi to Mom."

"Hey, where's your little brother?"

"Probably out back digging to China."

"Oh, still?"

"Yep."

"You Jeopard kids. Both diggers. I wonder what that's about."

CHAPTER 4

Chance leaned against the muddy wall of his hole and studied his letter in the growing dark. It was an ordinary-looking envelope, now very dirty, with an address, a return address, and a vermilion postage stamp with an intricately line-engraved bust of a strange creature, darkly canceled. The letter was thin, probably just a single folded sheet inside. The postage stamp was from some unrecognizable foreign country and denominated in *clahd*, a currency Chance, an enthusiastic numismatist, had never heard of. But the address was in English, in handwriting worse than his own:

Patient 251987
Saint Philomene's Infirmary
for Magical Creatures
Basement, #299
4211 Pipe C330649
Level Two, Slice 1401.812
Donbaloh

And the return address:

Fallor Medoby Dox
20002 Pipe R001213
Level One, Slice 60.996
Oppabof

What the . . . ? How Chance wished he could google those names and places, but he was not yet allowed to have internet access in his room—that was a privilege he was hoping for on his thirteenth birthday, still four months away. The passwords to his mother's desktop and his sister's laptop had thus far completely defeated him. The only internet access was at Jiro's.

"Whatcha doin' down there," said a pair of voices in unison.

"Augh!" shrieked Chance, turning quickly and hiding the letter behind his back. In the gloom above him, he noted the face of his annoying sister and the divine visage of Mersey Marsh. "Nothing!"

"You look like you've been, um, digging," said Pauline.

"Nope!"

"What have you got behind your back?" said Mersey, her sweet voice fluttering down into the hole like lace butterflies and landing on his head and face. *What the heck is wrong with me?*

"Not a thing!" said Chance.

"Suuuure," said Pauline. "C'mon, Merse. Let's go."

At bedtime, after his second bath of the day, Chance put on his pajamas, then sat on the edge of the bed and held the begrimed envelope up to the bulb of his bedside lamp. He could make out writing inside, but no words. He tucked the envelope under his pillow and turned out his light. He lay there for what seemed like hours. He was conscious of Mersey and Pauline in the next room, also not sleeping but, rather, watching what Chance recognized from its timbre and tone as an episode of *Battlestar Galactica*. The girls giggled sometimes, and once or twice they laughed out loud. Chance kind of wished he was in there with them, a party to their secrets, but that would never happen: He was officially a *bratty little brother*.

The letter under his head seemed to be screaming right

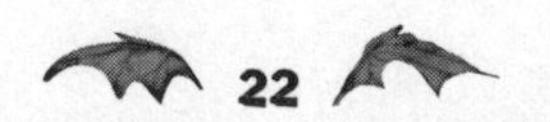

through the pillow: *Open me!* What Chance thought he *should* do is go to sleep, get up early in the morning, drop the letter back in the pipe, and let the wind carry it to Saint Philomene's Infirmary for Magical Creatures, whatever *that* was, and then plug up the jagged little hole with a tennis ball, climb out, and spend the day shoveling dirt back into the hole.

But what Chance *did* do was this: tiptoe downstairs to the kitchen, quietly fill the kettle with water, turn on the burner, and wait for what seemed like eons until steam finally began to flare from the spout. Water boiling in a steel kettle, even a non-whistling kettle, was awfully loud. And his mother, just down the hall in the downstairs bedroom, was a light sleeper. This needed to be done *quick*.

He stuck the envelope in the cone of steam. *So noisy!* His mother was going to wake up. Or, worse, Pauline would come downstairs for a bowl of Count Chocula. Or Mersey Marsh, in the mood for a baloney sandwich, might wander in wearing one of Pauline's nightgowns. That would undo Chance.

Steam, hurry!

An edge of the flap on the envelope suddenly popped up. The stickum was slowly melting. Eventually, the flap separated altogether. Chance slid the letter out of the envelope.

My dearest friend,

Your last letter worried me.

What is that? Footsteps? Chance turned off the burner, raced upstairs as silently as he could, slipped into his room, and jumped into bed, where he held his breath and tried to will his heart to stop elbowing its way out of his chest. When all was quiet, and he could hear nothing but Mersey and Pauline murmuring, he unfolded the mysterious missive.

CHAPTER 5

B*attlestar Galactica* ended, and Pauline picked up her fulgurite again. It had a root, or maybe a trunk, that branched out into five limbs, each of which bore numerous twigs, and from these "grew" even smaller twigs, each tapering to a dull point. The fulgurite was hollow, and its inside walls were glassy and smooth, like the mouth of a conch shell. It took up about as much space as a regulation basketball.

Mersey opened up Pauline's planet-sticker-covered laptop.

"Let's research it," she said. "What's your password again?"

"Gninthgil."

Mersey typed *fulgurite magic* into Google and was immediately rewarded with 78,140 hits.

"Hah!" she said. "Look, fulgurites are used in spells, prayer, spiritual communication, and, when ground up and mixed with other stuff, they were used in medicine in the olden days. Like in the fifteenth century, doctors used them to treat the vapors."

"What are the vapors?" said Pauline.

"Freak-outs, hysteria," said Mersey, who was a walking dictionary of bygone words. "And here's a website that says it was used, back in the eleventh and twelfth centuries, to treat werewolf bites. And to heal limbs broken by demons or malevolent spirits."

"Ridiculous," said Pauline, but Mersey didn't seem to hear. Mersey Marsh usually did not hear what Mersey Marsh did not want to hear.

"And," continued Mersey, "it says they were used to communicate over long distances. Two pieces broken off the same fulgurite act kind of like walkie-talkies, no matter how far apart."

Pauline said, "We're sure not busting up my fulgurite to test it."

Mersey looked hurt.

It was Pauline's turn with the computer. A quick search revealed that big branched fulgurites, which were very fragile, were extremely rare and valuable. Pauline looked

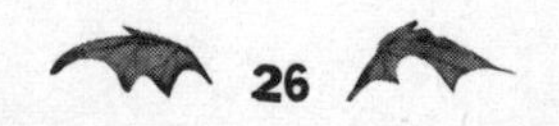

through all the images she could find. None were as beautiful as hers.

"It's a one of a kind," said Pauline.

"Let's bring it in to Dr. Kinfiggish."

Dr. Kinfiggish was the earth sciences teacher, whose class both the girls had taken. Mersey had sat directly behind Pauline. It was there that they had met and become friends.

The year before, during the fourth week of school, before they'd known each other, Mersey had passed a note written on yellow legal-pad paper folded into a Dorito-sized triangle to her future friend.

The note was in green ink and read:

Is Josh Ringle cute or what? I mean *really*.

Pauline had never in her life received a note in class. She didn't make friends easily, and when she did, the friendship was usually short-lived. She just didn't have much to say to the other kids. She was especially shy around her earth sciences classmate Josh Ringle, on whom she had pinned a great crush the first day of classes that grew with each passing day. Pauline didn't feel comfortable talking to her mother about boys, and, obviously, she couldn't talk to Chance—he was a child. But now, there was someone. And she was right behind her. Pauline was not alone with her crush.

Pauline wrote on the same piece of paper:

Omigosh, I know!

She carefully folded the paper back up, using the same creases, until it formed exactly the same triangle she had received, and passed it back.

Pauline could hear her classmate unfolding it; she could just barely hear the smooth rumble of the green ballpoint on the wooden desk; she could hear the soft crackling as Mersey refolded the paper. Then, Pauline felt a light tap on her shoulder. Beneath their first exchange, Pauline's new acquaintance had written:

I love his green eyes and black hair.

Pauline felt the same way and said so in the note, then folded it up and passed it back. This correspondence went on for the rest of the class. When the bell rang, Pauline was too shy to turn around and say hi, and the two went their separate ways.

Day after day, the two of them passed the note—the same piece of paper, which grew more and more crowded with confessions, opinions, declarations, and plots, many of these centering on oblivious Josh, until the paper was covered, *horror vacui*, in ink and pencil scratchings.

One Friday afternoon, in a space on the paper about two by twenty millimeters, Pauline wrote before passing the note:

Meet @ DQ aft sch?

Pauline felt something against her back, a small area of pressure like the dull end of a ballpoint pen.

OK!

And that started it. Dairy Queen became their favorite after-school hangout. They did homework, ate badly, played hangman, texted each other across the table, and discussed Josh. They discussed dozens of lesser boys, too, all cute in one way or another and each worthy of review, but none scored as high in so many categories as Josh Ringle.

Mersey and Pauline plotted ways to get his attention, enumerated his good looks, remarked on his intelligence (he was a natural as far as the earth sciences went), and took secret photos of him. Mersey had one photo—a clear, zoomed-in profile—enlarged and printed as a poster, which she hung over her bed. From another photograph, Pauline painted in acrylic a miniature portrait on a tiny square of unstretched canvas. It was a fine likeness, and Mersey offered to trade her poster for it, but Pauline, as much as she loved Mersey, couldn't part with her tiny masterpiece. For months she kept it rolled up in an Altoids box in her top drawer, then finally put it in a small but tasteful wooden frame and displayed it on her dresser.

Now, months later, it still lay there as Pauline said to Mersey, "I was thinking I'd like to show Dr. Kinfiggish my fulgurite, but school's out and all, and he's probably happy to be away from all us kids."

"So what are you going to do with it?"

"Nothing, I guess," said Pauline, yawning like a canyon. "Maybe just put it on my dresser."

Pauline stood up and did exactly that. It became the centerpiece among a collection of knickknacks—a miniature operational printing press, a black leather folding case with a photo of her great-great-great-grandfather in his Civil War uniform, a small box of real arrowheads, a contrivance of magnets organized in such a way that a ball bearing suspended over them hovered in midair, and, of course, the tiny portrait of Josh.

There was a knock on the door. Pauline scrambled up onto her bed and jumped under the covers while Mersey sheathed herself in a sleeping bag on the floor.

"Is it your mom?" whispered Mersey. "Are we up too late?"

"Who (*yawn*) is it (*yawn*)?" said Pauline, trying to sound sleepy.

"It's me, Chance!"

Pauline sat up and rolled her eyes. Sometimes her brother made her roll her eyes so hard they felt like they might get stuck in her head.

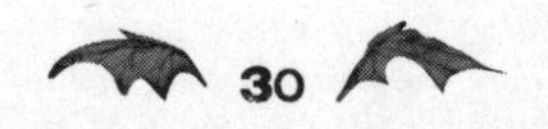

"What is it? Want to say hi to Mersey?"

Mersey threw a pillow at her friend.

"I have to show you guys something!"

"We're asleep," said Pauline, tossing the pillow back at Mersey, who caught it with one hand and fired it back, scoring a direct face hit on Pauline.

"No, I heard you giggling," said Chance.

"You can *hear* us?"

"Sure," Chance whispered through the door. "You watched *Battlestar Galactica*, opened two sodas, listened to a Daniel Johnston record—"

"Don't spy on us, sibling," said Pauline, throwing a smaller, decorative pillow at her friend, which caught her on the temple. Mersey frisbeed it back just as Pauline hurled the big pillow.

"I'm not spying; you're just so loud I can't sleep. Look, guys, I have to show you this thing I have!"

"You can't come in, Chance. Show me tomorrow. I have something to show you, too. We'll do show-and-tell and eat Count Chocula in the morning."

"Can I borrow your computer then? And will you give me your password?"

"Not a chance, Chance!"

Mersey stood up, holding the big pillow by a corner, then came toward Pauline, swinging the pillow over her head like a mace. She was about to peg her friend on the side

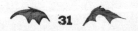

of the head when the pillow flew out of its case, whipped across the room, and knocked everything off Pauline's dresser—the Civil War photo, the printing press, the arrowheads, the magnetic toy, Josh's portrait, and, of course, the fulgurite, which fell to the hardwood floor with a glassy crunch, fracturing into dozens of pieces.

CHAPTER 6

Downstairs, Daisy was dreaming of a warm gray room filled ankle deep with water when a noise, at once loud but distant, startled her awake. She sat up, listening. A door slammed upstairs. Daisy grabbed a lamp, yanked out the plug, and proceeded up the stairs, her weapon poised above her head.

"Chance?" she said. "Pauline?"

No sound. She opened the door to her daughter's room. "Girls?"

"Yes, Mom?" said a fake-sleepy-sounding Pauline.

"Yes, Mrs. Jeopard?" said a fake-sleepy-sounding Mersey.

"What was that noise?"

"What noise?"

"It was . . . oh, never mind. Go to sleep."

Daisy shut the door and peeked into her son's room. He was sound asleep. She went around the upstairs, checking doors and closets and windows. Satisfied, she headed back downstairs. On the last step, she trod upon a piece of paper, which stuck to her foot. It tore when she removed it. An envelope, dirty, empty. She tossed it in the recycling bin, then checked the doors and windows downstairs and went back to her room.

CHAPTER 7

Chance could not sleep. The open letter lay on his bedside table. He could not be alone with this. *Why won't Pauline let me in*? he wondered. She would know what to do. She was just flaunting her older-sister prerogative in front of Mersey. Oh well. He turned on his light and read the letter again.

My dearest friend,

Your last letter worried me. I cannot believe the infirmary is in such imminent danger, yet I believe you; I have never had any reason to doubt you. That more than 1,800,000 patients' and staff members' lives are in the hands of one fool sickens me. Saint Philomene's Infirmary for Magical Creatures is 955 years old, yes? My life has twice been saved there. I owe it at least a defense.

But I cannot travel by pipe any longer; I am too old. One of my wings has even broken off—the first sign of true feebleness, at least for my kind. I can only send this letter, which is accompanied by a powerful philter. No, there is no vial contained herein; the chemical is instead invested in the paper. Yes, the chemical is <u>in</u> the paper.

To release it, do this: With your hands, press this sheet into a small ball, as small as strength will allow. Place the ball in a glass, and add just enough water to cover it. Wait two hours, remove the paper, and discard it (the writing will have washed out), add twelve drops of your own blood to the water—no more, no less—wait another two hours, then boil away the water until there is but a thimbleful left. This is flerk. Flerk is a catholicon, capable of curing many infirmities. It was at one time plentiful, but Saint Philomene's depleted all known sources decades ago. I only happen to be in possession of the little within this paper through the probated will of my grandfather, who died last month, leaving me a cabinet of medica curiosa. With the quantity of flerk you will soon possess, you will be at the yoke of a great healing force. Though it will not cure a fool of anything, you could use the flerk to relieve a Giant Cpulba of any cancer; rescue an Unman from the kenicki-quithers; banish terminal brain fulse from a wandering Tepesette; free a Werewolf of Hurlworm; or save a scuttling Brux from insanity.

Alas, there is not nearly enough to save 1,800,000 beings, my dear Simon, but in your hands, it could save the one capable of saving the all.

Your ever-faithful servant,
Fallor Medoby Dox

Werewolves! Could they be for real? And what in the world were Brux? And Giant Cpulba? Chance knew he never should have stuck his arm in the dang pipe. Why hadn't he listened to his conscience? Some underworld realm was going to perish because of him. Wait, there weren't any underground realms . . . were there? But the letter seemed so *real*. And so he knew he must restore it to its journey. Right now.

He quietly dressed in Wranglers, a Möbius strip T-shirt, and dirt-caked Keds.

Chance wasn't exactly *afraid* of the dark, but if given a choice of climbing in a seven-and-a-half-foot hole at midday or at midnight, it was a no-brainer. All he had to do was roll up the letter and pop it back in the hole, then run back to bed. The letter would've lost only a few hours' transit time; surely, no "beings" would die.

He folded the letter. Where was the envelope? Hmm. Not on the bedside table. Not under the covers. Not on the floor. Not under the bed. He must have dropped it coming up the stairs. He shut his bedroom door behind him and scanned the hallway floor.

But it wasn't anywhere. Not under the old, faded Shiraz carpet in the hall, not on the smooth wood stairs. He searched his room again, and then searched downstairs one more time. He even looked in places the envelope couldn't possibly be: kitchen drawers, the hall closet, the pile of mail on the sideboard by the front door.

He began to panic. He couldn't remember the address on the envelope, or even the addressee. *Patient something something. Pipe C33 something something. Slice 1401 point something something something . . . No! Dang it!* He simply could not remember. *Crud!* There would be blood on his hands. *What to do! Think!*

And there, in the middle of the upstairs hallway, at the witching hour on the first full official day of summer vacation, Chance realized what it was that he had to do.

He folded the letter and tucked it into the back pocket of his jeans, went into his room, put on his watch, then filled his pockets with a penknife, nine dollars, a magnifying glass, a compass, a small, powerful flashlight and extra AAA batteries, and a box of matches. Downstairs, he loaded an old satchel with two bottles of water, a jar of peanut butter, a package of soda crackers, Flintstones vitamins, and six of the Hershey's Nuggets with almonds his mother kept "hidden" in a kitchen drawer. Then he went outside, careful to close the sliding glass door as silently as he could, stole across the yard in the moonlight, and climbed into the hole. He picked up the shovel and began to quietly chip away at the gap in the pipe. *Choc, chup, chak, chip.* When the breach was wide enough to allow his body to pass through, he slipped inside and found himself on all fours, facing south, the powerful wind whipping the backs of his legs. The walls of the pipe were Teflon-smooth. He took a deep breath, innnn . . . ouuut . . . innnn . . . ouuut . . .

And Chance began to crawl.

CHAPTER 8

Pauline and Mersey stared at the scatter of fulgurite smithereens all over the room. Mersey clapped her hand over her mouth. She began to tear up.

A noise downstairs. *Mom!*

"Get in your sleeping bag," Pauline whispered as she jumped into her own bed. "Let's pretend we're asleep."

Outside the door, Pauline's mother said, "Chance? Pauline?"

The bedroom door opened.

"Girls?"

"Yes, Mom?" said Pauline, over-yawning.

"Yes, Mrs. Jeopard?" said Mersey, also yawning dramatically.

"What was that noise?"

"What noise?"

"It was . . . oh, never mind. Go to sleep."

She shut the door. Pauline and Mersey listened for her to go back downstairs. Then Mersey whispered, "Pauline, I'm sooooooo sorry about your . . . thing . . ."

Pauline said nothing for a moment.

"Pauline?"

"It's okay, Mersey. Really, it is. Just an accident. Help me put it back together?"

"Okay."

Pauline turned on the light. They collected all the fragments they could find and began to reassemble them, as if the fulgurite were a tiny, unknown species of dinosaur whose bones were discovered in disarray.

But one piece was missing. They searched the room again. And the hallway, because a piece could have skidded under the door. Nothing.

"That's okay," said Pauline. "The beauty is in the flaw. That's what Daddy would've said. Or something like it."

With a tube of cyanoacrylate, the girls began to glue the pieces back together. Some of the joins were almost invisible. It would be nearly as good as new.

Pauline held one piece back, the last piece, a slightly twisted reddish-gold tube about a pinkie's length and breadth whose smooth inside walls had the pearly translucence of green dish soap.

"Here," she said, handing it to her friend. "This is a good piece. You have it."

Mersey started to tear up again.

"Stop that now, Mersey Marsh," said Pauline, leaning over to hug her friend. "Let's get some sleep."

The girls climbed under their respective covers.

Pauline couldn't sleep. What exactly was so important that Chance had had to knock on her door? That was highly atypical. Lately, Chance went out of his way to avoid being around Mersey Marsh because the sight of her made him floppy and dense. That alone should have been enough to keep him away, but he'd still wanted to come in. Maybe he'd had something genuinely important to show her.

But it could wait till morning. Pauline fell asleep, dreaming of her intrepid, innocent little brother, of chandeliers falling from invisible ceilings, of boys made of rain, of vast gray blankets embroidered with squiggles of black and green thread.

The girls didn't wake up until eleven the next morning. Chance was nowhere around.

"Let's go to Dairy Queen and have ice cream for breakfast," said Mersey, who was doing her makeup in the mirror of Pauline's little green vanity, a bit of children's furniture that had so far survived the purges of adolescence. "And a popcorn shrimp basket."

"Hey, can I try your fangs?"

"Sure. But they probably won't fit."

Pauline stuck the two ceramic fangs on her canines. Not perfect, but they stayed in place. They looked quite real.

"Wow," said Mersey.

"Can I wear them today?"

"Sure."

At a table outside the DQ, a peanut butter sundae and popcorn shrimp basket between them, Mersey and Pauline watched for boys. Specifically, for Josh Ringle, who occasionally dropped in for a chocolate-dipped cone and a bit of texting.

But no luck. Pauline, in a way, was relieved. Something about the existence of Josh, even though it had been the mortar of their friendship, was now beginning to throw up a barrier between herself and Mersey. At least it was summer vacation now, and all three of them weren't in class together. Even though the classroom had seated forty-five people, in the end it had begun to feel too small for the three of them.

Mersey's phone rang, its ringtone the somber beat of Bauhaus's "Bela Lugosi's Dead."

"Hello? Oh, hi, Mom. Dairy Queen. You know, ice cream. She's fine. Aw, Mom, do I have to? Why? Uncle Dob isn't going to be there, is he? Well, he's not bringing his puppets, I hope. He is? Great. Okay, okay, I'll be home in an hour." Mersey hung up.

"What . . . ?"

"Family barbecue," said Mersey. "Wanna come?"

"Okay," said Pauline, who didn't mind puppet shows at all and liked barbecued chicken a lot.

Mersey's phone rang again. Pauline stared at it. So did Mersey. Then she picked up.

"Hello? Yes? Um, this is she. Oh, uh, hi. Um, from Kinfiggish's? Oh sure, I remember. Yeah, school sucks. Ha-ha-ha!"

Mersey stood up and walked over to a nearby cedar. Pauline struggled to hear, but the traffic on Loblolly Road drowned it out. Pauline watched as Mersey's posture changed from straight to swayey to slouchy to slinky. She was blushing, obvious even under all the makeup. Finally, Mersey hung up and came back to the table.

"You won't believe who that was," she said.

"Who?" said Pauline, knowing all too well who it was.

"Josh Ringle."

"No."

"Yep, he asked me out. Tomorrow night. A date. To see *Buzzard People* at the Downtown Bijou. He has a car!"

"Incredible, wow."

"He said he'd been crushing on me all year."

"That's great."

"Yeah."

"Think your mom will let you go?" Pauline said.

"No, that's why I'm not going to tell her. I'm going to say I'm staying late at your house. Um, if that's okay?"

"Sure."

"I'll have Josh drop me off at your house afterward, and I'll throw pebbles at your window."

"Fine."

"Pauline, are you okay with me going on a date with him?"

"Sure."

"I don't believe you. You look a little upset."

"I always look a little upset."

"Not true."

"Mersey, seriously, I'm cool with it. I want you to have fun on your date without worrying about me."

Pauline looked down at the table, at its old cracks and carved initials, at the line of ants climbing the shrimp basket, at the bee skimming the chaos of a half-finished peanut butter sundae melting in the meridian Texas sun.

CHAPTER 9

Daisy woke up late to an empty house. Pauline had left a note on the kitchen counter:

DQ, bk sn, ♡ P.

Chance was not in the habit of leaving notes and often went off early to raise some kind of minor hell, always returning in the evening covered in dirt and grass stains, so his absence did not surprise her.

Pauline came in through the sliding glass door.

"Hi, sweetie. Where's Mersey?"

"I don't care," said Pauline.

"Hm. Well, I just wanted to remind you I'm going to Denver tomorrow morning. I'll be gone a few days."

"You're not going to have Pye babysit us again, are you?"

"No, no. If you need anything, go get Mrs. Applebaker. I let her know you two will be by yourselves. Where's your little brother?"

"I'm sure he's off doing something risky and simple-minded."

"Well," said Daisy. "You might be right. Yesterday he told me he's sleeping over at Jiro's tonight."

"Yay for Chance."

"Be sweet."

CHAPTER 10

Dave Green, possibly the crankiest man in all of Lubbock, Texas, locked up the secret government laboratory where he labored as a biochemist developing agents of biological warfare for the US military, then climbed into his new Chevy pickup, drove to his house on the north side of town, and fell diagonally across his bed without undressing. Dave Green was very ill.

Some weeks before, he had caught a disease in his lab after accidentally sticking himself in the thumb with a hypodermic. The symptoms came quickly. It was a rare disease known to science only by the designation JENCKX30, and invulnerable to medicine. Dave had been working on a cure most of his adult life, using the same laboratory in which he developed horrifying bugs of mass destruction. That he had, at age sixty-one, caught the same disease that killed his grandmother fifty years before scared him, enraged him, and brought him down all at once. Dave's grandmother, who had raised him since infancy after his parents were killed in a plane crash, died of the disease when he was eleven. Dave had vowed to find a cure.

In truth, Dave wasn't sure if his grandmother had died from JENCKX30 itself; she had mysteriously disappeared from the world before the symptoms overcame her. She had never been found. Dave had made biochemistry and medicine his course of study, and his life's work.

Dave didn't know how much longer he had. A week or so, maybe a bit more. Toward the very end, he would develop a high fever—the classic symptom that signaled the beginning of the end, the point at which one started counting one's remaining time in hours, not days.

But before the fever, there would come a much more troubling and disabling symptom. It would begin as simple confusion, then graduate to a kind of generic paranoia, and then progress to full-blown madness. It would start subtly and then accelerate. Thinking about it scared him.

Dave Green wanted to blame somebody. But there was no one; he could fault only himself.

When morning came, Dave drank some Sanka, then went on the internet to play chess, his only remaining pleasure.

Dave was a very skilled player. At least his mind still worked. He had a good, regular opponent, sleight_of_hand, who was a bit inferior to Dave, which was good, because Dave didn't want to spend the rest of his days *losing* at chess.

He signed on as virus_master and was satisfied to see that sleight_of_hand was available. In the dialogue box at the bottom of the screen appeared a greeting from SoH.

"How are you today, VM? Any better?"

"A little worse," typed Dave. "I don't think I have much time."

"I'm sorry to hear it. So. Let us begin. I take white this time, yes?"

"Sure."

SoH advanced a pawn two ranks. Dave blocked it with a pawn of his own, and a classic blow-parry-blow struggle for the center squares ensued, neither player wandering from textbook moves until SoH unexpectedly sacrificed a knight for two pawns at move 15, leaving Dave's king open to attack. SoH cunningly took the opportunity to chat.

"VM, what exactly are your symptoms? If I may be so bold?"

Dave did not respond. He was sweating and shivering at the same time. He had not seen the sacrifice coming. He went into the kitchen for a handful of pine nuts and a glass of milk. When he returned, he drew a knight back in front of his king, the only reasonable defense.

"Mainly, it's the shakes. Then there's blurred vision, intense hand spasms, and dry mouth."

"Hm. Really."

"And an illusory sense that one cannot stretch out one's legs. Most upsetting."

"Go on."

"But the most obvious and unique feature is the rash of greenish dots all over the skin. Small, sharply defined blemishes. They look like pencil-jab marks."

"Greenish, you say?" typed SoH, who then slipped a bishop into the long diagonal, straight at Dave's king.

"Yeah."

"Terminal, you say?"

"Yes."

"Strange," typed SoH.

"And," typed Dave Green, "you go nuts."

"I see." After a moment, SoH typed, "There is a similar disease here, where I live. But it's called GIGI."

"And you live where?"

Dave began a new skirmish line on the opposite side of the board, three pawns advancing on a trapped bishop.

"All in good time."

"Fine."

And there was no more communication until the end

of the game, which Dave won with an interminable rook versus rook-and-pawn endgame.

"A fine contest, VM."

"Thanks."

"I've been thinking. Where I live, there is a cure for GIGI, which I am certain is your ailment."

"Really."

Dave was in no mood for false hope.

"Perhaps you should come here. For treatment."

"Oh sure," typed Dave, with as much bitter humor as he could impart to the keys. "There *is* no treatment."

"What have you got to lose?"

"Okay," said Dave, pushing a pawn to the center of the board to begin the next game. "I'll try again: Where do you live?"

Silence again. Half the game was played, with no advantage for either side.

"If I tell you," typed SoH, "you must promise to never divulge it."

"Sure, whatever."

"Well. I, too, am ill. But there is no treatment for me, even though I live in a vast hospital. Underground."

"I always knew you were a nut."

"I am risking a great deal divulging this."

"Where?"

"Under Texas. Very few people, know about it."

"I'm laughing out loud."

"In 1968," said SoH, "a woman appeared here. She had this disease. It had never been seen before, and many hundreds were infected, and most died. But a remedy was quickly developed, using an enzyme discovered in the cells of the very few survivors."

"Ridiculous, ridiculous!" wrote Dave, though he wanted to believe.

"GIGI has never returned. Since then, though, the woman's kind has not been welcome here. In fact, they have been banned."

" 'Her kind'?"

"Yes. Hard to explain."

"Sure it is. Okay, I'll play along. Why is it called GIGI?"

"It's named after the woman who brought it here. It stands for Georgette Inchbald Green's Infirmity."

Dave Green froze. His grandmother's name! Had . . . had she somehow wound up . . . *there*? This was impossible to believe. This crazy person was running some kind of scam. Dave shook his head hard, causing his thin hair to rise in brief oscillations. Or . . . this was the beginning. The beginning of the insanity.

"And," typed Dave, "what happened to her?"

"She was remanded to a quarantined prison cell, where she was forgotten . . . and died, of neglect. It was a shameful day for the infirmary."

"I don't ever want to hear from you again."

Dave Green slammed his laptop shut.

That night, he slept even worse than he had the night before. Restless, nonstop half dreams of his grandmother falling into mine shafts; of gigantic pencils stabbing his hands; of being trapped in his lab, thigh deep in a Gobi of deadly viral powders, flailing and holding his breath; of pawns with the power of two queens and chessboards made of solar flares; of fury in the guise of calm; of despair; of vengeance. Of madness.

At 4:30 a.m., Dave signed on to ChessKnight.com, where he quickly found sleight_of_hand.

"Okay," wrote Dave. "How do I get there?"

And, against all rational inquiry, Dave Green dressed in the disguise described by SoH, got in his Chevy, parked behind a nearby Albertsons, locked his truck, and, at 9:31:07 a.m., climbed into a Dumpster and waited.

CHAPTER 11

The pipe was as dark as a blacksmith's basement. Chance crawled slowly along the slick surface, his body just barely fitting. Behind him, the wind pushed at him like a linebacker. The little flashlight, as powerful as it was, illumined only twenty feet in front of him; beyond that, oblivion.

This is craziness! What am I doing? It could be a thousand miles! Chance stopped for a moment. He'd been traveling for an hour. It was almost four in the morning. There wasn't room to turn around; he was going to have to crawl backward to get home. He would keep going for three more hours, then reassess.

A new possibility struck him on the side of the head like a cold fish: What if it started to rain? What if it rained hard, like yesterday? There might be mud. Lots. He pictured it oozing into the pipe, piling high, eventually blocking the hole off. He could die here. Dying was not in Chance's plans.

But the beings, whatever they were, what about them? He wished Pauline were here. She would know what to do. On the other hand, she probably wouldn't believe any of this business of flerk and kenicki-quithers and 955-year-old hospitals. She would scoff.

Chance continued on. It was getting hotter, and the pipe now declined at an ever-so-shallow angle. What if it got steeper and steeper, and he lost his grip on the surface and began to luge toward hell?

Something spanked him on the rear end and stuck there. *Ow! What the heck? Oh, it must be a piece of mail.* It felt funny, sticking to his butt like that, the wind holding it in place, but there wasn't room to reach back and remove it.

Thap! Another piece of mail landed on top of the first. *Lup!* Another! Then *kop, sip, slup, fipflit,* letter after letter hitting him in the butt and the backs of his legs, some slipping between him and the walls and shooting on down the pipe, but most amassing behind him, a drift of paper against his body that threatened to grow so large it would clog the pipe, stop the engine of wind altogether, and prevent him from ever returning home.

But this did not happen. Instead, Chance found himself

being gently propelled by the wind along the pipe like a red cell in a capillary, moving no faster than he'd been crawling. This was a rather pleasant change, as he was awash in perspiration and his kneecaps hurt.

The wind blew him and his big clot of mail along like a schooner. Chance was traveling a bit faster now. And now faster. Soon, there was no stopping; Chance tried to dig the heels of his hands into the pipe, but it felt like a nonstick frying pan. They were traveling at the pace of a brisk walk. Now it was a leisurely jog; now a lazy streetcar ride; now they were running to catch the bus; now they were Usain Bolt, the friction heating his shins through his jeans; now they were on an airboat in the east Texas swamps, racing past alligators and cypress trees; and now they were on a Moto Guzzi going over the speed limit on a straight two-lane road on the coastal plains; and now they were on a rocket sled on the Bonneville Salt Flats; and now they were within a whisper of the sound barrier. . . . For almost an hour, Chance hurtled through this underground tube on his way to deliver a letter—no mailman had ever done this!—to some *thing* he wasn't sure existed in a place that might be no place at all, all for no good reason except to stanch a gush of guilt and quell the feeling he would be failing his dead father if he didn't. Then Chance noticed something ahead of him: a tiny white dot, a quark of light, in the center of the circle of dark distance before him, and it slowly grew and grew until it was the size of a dime, then a nickel, growing until it was like staring into the beam of a flashlight, now the disc of the full moon, now . . . light was all around him, a blare of whiteness and fluttering. And he tumbled through space in a maelstrom of mail until gravity snatched him and dashed him onto the pile of letters in what he would later learn was Saint Philomene's Infirmary for Magical Creatures Sorting Room M40 (Incoming), a white box of a hundred feet along every dimension. The bottom twenty feet was filled with unsorted mail destined for the patients and staff of the last place on earth where, as Chance would also learn, certain of the world's inhabitants—fairies, demigods, barrow-wights, zombies, vizards, kraken, ouphes, superheroes, vampires, and others, so many others—could go if their bodies were being eaten by disease or their minds by melancholy or their population by viruses, because no terrestrial hospitals would know what to do with them. Saint Philomene's Infirmary for Magical Creatures was where they went because there was nowhere else to go.

Chance was soon to learn that Saint Philomene's did *not* welcome humans.

CHAPTER 12

Pauline idled over her dinner, moving the peas one at a time to make a circle around the mashed potatoes. She was still full from the barbecue, during which she had not seen much of Mersey, who had spent most of her time inside trying on outfits and doing her brows for her date tomorrow night.

"Where's Chance?" said Pauline. She thought maybe she *would* talk to her brother about Mersey and Josh Ringle, about what happened today at the DQ, since Pauline didn't want to tell her mother about it. Pauline got the feeling her mother had never much liked Mersey Marsh and would be sort of happy if she disappeared from her daughter's life. And it appeared that that was in fact what was happening: Mersey had not sent photos of herself in her chosen outfit as she'd promised.

"He's probably at Jiro's," said Daisy. "He's going to spend the night. Remember?"

The phone rang. Pauline jumped up from the table to get it. Oh. Not Mersey. It was from Jiro's house. Probably Chance calling. She didn't want to talk to her brother on the phone, especially in front of her mother. She let it go to voice mail. She stared at the phone for a moment, considering calling Mersey. The screen on the phone went black, and Pauline was suddenly staring at her reflection in the glass. Omigosh, she was still wearing Mersey's fangs. Pauline surreptitiously plucked them off and tucked them into a jeans pocket. Had her Mom seen them? She must not have, or she would've said something.

"Mom, I'm going to my room."

"Okay, sweetie."

Pauline got on the internet and searched *Josh Ringle* (if only she knew his middle name!), like she'd done a gazillion times before. As always, there was a mention of his .360 batting average in Little League two years ago, a group photo of his third-grade class, and a mention as a survivor in an obituary for Clyde Ringle, Josh's grandfather. From this same obit, Pauline learned his parents' names and that he had two sisters, Judy and Serena. Other bytes of info came from searching his name misspelled: *Ringall, Ringel, Ringles.* Pauline was a clever Googler and knew, among many other tricks, to search his name as it would be listed in a phonebook: *Ringle, Josh.*

But there was never anything new.

Pauline woke up at ten the next morning, went downstairs with her glued-together fulgurite in one hand, and finished off the box of cereal. She watched the clock. Chance would be home soon.

Tonight was Mersey's date with Josh.

Daisy came out of her room.

"Is your little brother home from Jiro's yet?" she said. "He has chores to attend to. I told him this would be the Summer of Labor. Besides, I want to say good-bye."

"Haven't seen his little troll face in a while."

"Pauline."

"Sorry. What time are you leaving?"

"Flight to Denver's at one; I'm headed out in just a minute. Back in a week. All the numbers are on the Paper."

The Paper was an eleven-by-seventeen sheet of paper, more than twenty years old, covered with phone numbers and contact information. It was stained, wrinkled, dirty, sacred, eminently useful, irreplaceable.

"Okay."

"I called Jiro's, but no one answered," said Daisy. "Maybe

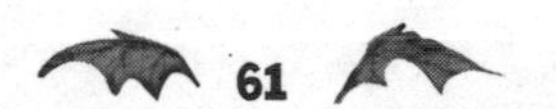

they're out having breakfast. Now, you'll be all right by yourself, and you'll watch Chance. Right?"

"I will."

"Good. Call Jiro's again later and ask Chance to call me immediately."

Daisy said, more to herself than to Pauline, that Chance was an industrious and unpredictable sweetheart and there was no need for concern. But Pauline noticed a shade of worry in her mother's face, which made Pauline worry a bit herself. But her mother was odd. Sometimes she behaved as if she lived in a bubble with a population of one: herself.

Pauline waved from the driveway as Daisy drove off.

Still no word from Mersey.

Pauline paced around her room. Why wouldn't Mersey call? Then Pauline thought that she should call Mersey, like she'd promised herself she'd do. But she wasn't ready.

She had to do *something* to keep herself busy.

She noticed Mersey's sleeping bag still on the floor. She rolled it up and put it in her closet. What a mess in there. Pauline sat on the floor and started pulling things out. *Cleaning*. Cleaning would keep her occupied. She pulled out an aluminum baseball bat, a bent telescope, millions of old shoes, a magic set, a two-foot-high stack of board games, dirty clothes, an empty bag of Fritos, a full bag of Fritos (that expired three years before), a menagerie of stuffed animals, and dust bunnies like tumbleweeds.

Pauline cleaned out the entire closet, swept,

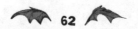

unsentimentally threw things away, then dusted off and re-placed everything she wanted to keep. When she was finished, she cleaned under her bed, picked all the clothes up off her floor, and neatened her dresser drawers. She vacuumed, keeping the phone in one hand so she'd know if it rang. She did five loads of laundry. Finally, she Windexed the downstairs TV, which she planned to watch until late. And did.

She fell asleep on the couch.

She had forgotten to call Jiro's.

In the morning she remembered. She ran to the phone. First, she listened to the message from two nights ago. It was Jiro's mother.

"Hi, Daisy. Akiko here. Listen, don't send Chance over to spend the night—Jiro came down with the throw-ups, and it looks like an all-nighter. Ciao!"

Chance hadn't even *been* at Jiro's. He'd been unaccounted for, for two nights! She felt like slapping herself on the cheek. *Bad sister!*

Pauline ran upstairs to Chance's room. He wasn't there. And his bed was unmade. Chance always made his bed. It was one of the only chores he performed faithfully. He claimed to like it.

Pauline hurried outside and raced to the backyard. No Chance, just a deep hole.

Pauline jogged next door to Mrs. Applebaker's house.

"Oh dear, I haven't seen him for a while," shc said. "It's

supposed to be a secret, but he borrowed my shovel a while back. That's the last I've seen of him."

Pauline walked back home. Where could he have gone? What had he wanted to show her? Did he find it in the hole? If she'd let him in when he knocked the other night, would he be home safe now? What was he doing right this minute?

Pauline began to really worry.

CHAPTER 13

Chance was covered in letters. Literally buried. He lifted his head, broke through a layer of mail, and peeked out. He was in a huge white room filled with letters, millions of them. Thousands of holes in the ceiling and every wall, each spitting out envelopes and parcels and magazines that rained down on Chance. In the center of the room, a huge crane hovered over the hills of mail, a big, rusty mechanical claw hanging from its crossarm by a chain. Not ten feet from him, Chance watched the claw open, drop into the piles of letters, grasp thousands at once, and slowly deposit its load into a vast aluminum hopper that funneled the letters into piles on a rapid conveyor belt that disappeared into a hole in one wall. Chance noticed a long window above the conveyor belt, through which he saw three creatures who were each standing at a console of sorts, pushing buttons, moving levers, turning dials. The creatures were like nothing he'd ever seen. Ten feet tall at least, they looked like huge pigs standing upright, but each was covered with thick, coarse fur—one red, one orange, one brownish yellow—and atop their turtlelike heads were perched small conical hats that looked as if they were made of rainbow taffy. They had long, knobby legs and wore shiny patent-leather boots in colors matching their fur. He would soon learn these creatures were called Vyrndeets.

Chance had gone insane. He was certifiable. He had lost his marbles. He was mad as a hatter, nutty as a fruitcake. He had fallen out of the crazy tree and hit every branch on the way down. Or was he dreaming? Seeing the future? Dead?

But what if he was perfectly alive, awake, in the present moment, sane, and all around him were truth and fact? Chance decided he needed to operate on this assumption. He shook his head and squeezed his eyes shut. When he opened them again, nothing had changed. Mail, mail, mail.

The beasts were supernaturally ugly, vicious looking, and, even at this distance, smelled powerfully of boiled broccoli.

Chance buried his head back under the letters. He

hadn't bargained on this. He had absolutely no idea what to do. Those beings looked like they'd eat him on a cracker.

He began to swim. So to speak. He scuttled under a layer of letters, slowly so he would not be noticed, toward the hole the conveyor belt went through. Every now and then he'd peek up between the layers of mail to check his progress. He was getting close. As long as that claw didn't come down and bite him in half. His heart beat like a two-stroke engine.

A loud, screechy alarm went off, a little like a fire drill in school, except sharper and more urgent. He looked out from under his letter-blanket. Gad! One of those creatures was staring right back at him with its pupilless, matte-black eyes, which looked like huge olives. Then, with a short, cloven-hoofed foreleg, it pointed at Chance. Chance jumped out from under the letters and began to make his way to the conveyor belt door, slipping, sliding, falling, and getting back up again. Still a dozen yards from what he hoped was freedom, Chance slipped again and landed on his back. He looked up. Directly above him, the huge, rusty claw was moving into position. It dropped. Chance rolled out of the way, the claw *thunk*ing into the mail inches away from him. Chance tried to scream, but it came out as a hiss. The claw began to rise back into the air; the jackbooted pig-turtles were clearly preparing to drop it on him again. Chance continued to roll, making much better time than he had on his feet. Before long, he was jumping onto the conveyor belt and on his way out of that infernal room, with its murderous mutant mailmen.

Chance found himself in near darkness, frightened, surrounded by the churning of machines, with the terrible alarm still sounding. As he became accustomed to the low light, he realized he was in a room with dozens of greasy sorting machines that looked like they'd churn him into ground-up Chance. He leaped off the belt onto a cement floor covered in old mail. In one corner of the room was a closed door made of riveted steel plates; in another was a chain dropping to the floor from a narrow hole in the ceiling thirty feet above. Chance didn't know if either led to freedom, but he was sure they at least led away from the three monsters, who would surely be coming after him. He rushed for the door. Just when he was only a few feet away, it opened, and a dozen round Saint Bernard–sized creatures with whippy antennae as long as they were tall burst in, each carrying a long, sharp halberd and a lead-weighted net.

"By the ghost of Saint Philomene, it's a human!" shouted one of them in a voice that reminded Chance of those singing chipmunks from TV. One tossed a net, and another tossed a halberd. Both landed well short of their terrified human target.

Chance ran for the chain. He began to climb. Halberds clanged on the walls, just barely missing him, and nets wrapped around his body, then slipped off and fell to the ground. Chance was nearly at the hole in the ceiling when a halberd pierced the hem of his shirt, barely missing his flesh, but pinning him to the wall. Frantically, he worked at the halberd with one hand. Two of the little round creatures began to climb up, each with a dagger between its teeth.

Only a few hours earlier, Chance had been lying in bed, his sister and Mersey Marsh in the room next door, his mother downstairs. They were still in bed, probably; it was only six a.m. there. *There.* Where was he now? How far away? How far *beneath*? He'd never be able to deliver the letter, the secret catholicon of flerk, which no one knew he had.

Hmm. . . .

He looked down at the climbing beings and shouted, "I have flerk! A cure-all! Just don't kill me!"

Incredulous, high-pitched titters erupted from the little creatures below.

"Flerk! Sure you do! Ha-ha-ha! You can't fool a Balliope, human!"

Chance looked over his shoulder. Bursting into the room were more of the spherical beings—Balliopes, evidently—except these were carrying pistols of some kind. One of them paused, leveled its weapon, and fired.

There was a chattery whir, then a sudden *jinth!* as a steel dart with wires tailing out of it stuck in the wall next to Chance's head. Chance, sweating and in a panic, worked at the halberd pinning him. Another electrified dart stuck in the wall near his leg. Finally, the halberd came loose and clattered to the floor. Chance scurried up the chain and into the hole in the ceiling. Right behind him were the two dagger-wielding Balliopes. The chain was hooked to a manual winch bolted to the floor. He yanked on the hand brake and the chain began to unwind, eventually slipping off altogether and falling down the hole. There were screams below: the two Balliopes crashing to the floor. Nobody could climb up now. He was safe, at least for the moment.

He looked around. He was in a vast, dark open space, like a warehouse, lit here and there with faint bulbs hanging on long cords that were swaying in a gentle breeze of unknown origin. The ceiling was at least five stories above, almost invisible in the gloom. Ladders, ducts, beams, poles, ramps, chutes, chains, and ropes, all rusty or mildewy or dirty or busted, crisscrossed the huge metal cavern. Overturned barrels as big as hay bales sat motionless here and there. Near the center of the space was a kind of large, squarish column rising all the way to the ceiling, like a chimney. Chance ran toward it. They'd be there soon. Minutes. Seconds, even. He trotted toward the chimney thing, careful not to trip on the many obstacles on the floor—abandoned wrenches, oily rags, broken planks, concrete shards, wheelbarrows, unidentifiable garbage, even a chest of drawers, and, by the strange column, a skeleton. A full human skeleton, tatters of leathery skin stretched across the bones. It had obviously been there a long, long time. Chance was proud of himself for not shrieking. He was growing hardier. He was, of course, either dead, dreaming, or insane, but very hardy indeed.

Or maybe it *was* all real. If so, he *would* survive it. He would not become a forgotten skeleton. He *would* save the beings, even though he had not much liked the ones he'd met so far.

The column was five feet on each side and apparently completely seamless. It appeared to actually come up through the floor, rather than stand upon it. Chance walked around it.

On the far side was a pair of double doors. A very familiar type of door with a pair of barely illuminated buttons next to it, each covered in dirt and the entropy of disuse, but labels that could be read: UP and DOWN.

Up seemed the sensible direction. He pushed the button and heard a groan from somewhere way, way below. It sounded like a huge steel pipe being bent in half by an ogre—not an implausible scenario in this place.

Chance heard shouts and grunts and yodels: They were getting closer. In a far corner, a door opened, flooding the place with light that danced with the shadows of his pursuers, far more of them than before. The elevator doors yawned open and he jumped in, hit the CLOSE DOORS button, and scanned the bank of numbers.

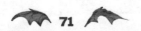

Apparently, he was on the 1,509th floor. *Wha . . . ?!* The tallest building in the world, the Burj Khalifa, in Dubai, only has 174, and that's if you count the maintenance levels in the spire and the two floors of underground parking! But fifteen *hundred* floors?

Chance shook his head vigorously. *Focus!* The elevator only went to the 1,212th floor—all the other numbers went up; Chance guessed that the lower the number, the closer to the surface of the Earth he was. If each floor was ten feet, Chance calculated he was almost three *miles* beneath the surface of the Earth. This was *impossible.* Wasn't it? He hit the 1,212th floor button. The elevator rose, slowly picking up speed.

What if they were waiting for him on 1,212? Chance decided to get off sooner. He waited until he was just below the 1,290th floor, then hit the button. The elevator jostled and rattled to an uneven stop.

The doors opened.

CHAPTER 14

Pauline sat in the kitchen and began to call all of Chance's friends. Vishy Chandry, Randy Kane, Jessamyne Zee, Harold Boyd, Jamal Rice, others. None had seen him.

Pauline knocked on all the neighbors' doors up and down her street, then down the parallel and cross streets. Hours later she walked home, where she found an old, rusted-out El Camino she immediately recognized as the property of a certain cousin of hers. What was *he* doing here? She groaned. Then she thought, *Maybe he's with Chance!*

She ran inside to find Pye McAllister sitting at the kitchen table, eating her new box of Count Chocula.

"Where's Chance?"

"No idea," said Pye.

"And what are you doing here? No offense."

"Your mama called me this morning and asked me to come by and watch y'all."

"Why? She said we didn't need a babysitter."

"She said she'd heard a noise in the house a couple nights ago, and it made her nervous, and that she would feel better if I was here for the duration."

"I'm too old for a babysitter."

"And yet here I am."

Pauline tried calling Mersey, but only reached her voice mail. She didn't leave a message.

Pye burped grandly, got up, and lay down on the couch to play *Death Galaxy Throwdown*.

"Polly, I'm still hungry. Why don't you make your old cousin Pye a cheese sandwich?"

"You haven't seen my brother since you got here?"

"No. Sandwich?"

Pauline hurriedly unwrapped three slices of American cheese, spread some mayo on a couple slices of wheat bread, added lettuce and tomato, and brought it to him with some chips on a paper plate.

"When I'm finished," said Pye, "I'm gonna nap right here, so don't disturb me."

Pauline ignored him. She picked up the three plastic

cheese wrappers and threw them in the recycling bin. She picked up the bin and hiked out to the alley. She was about to dump it all in the big blue barrel when she noticed a strange thing in the bin she was carrying. A stamp. Affixed to a letter. It was a postage stamp like none she'd ever seen before. On an envelope with strange addresses. No letter inside. She brought it into the house.

Did this have anything to do with Chance? She ran upstairs and dragged out her laptop. Searching *Saint Philomene's Infirmary for Magical Creatures* brought no hits. She also searched *Patient 251987, Fallor Medoby Dox,* and *Pipe C330649.* She experimented with variant spellings, word orders, etc. She looked up *infirmary* in foreign dictionaries and searched those spellings: *L'infirmerie de Philomène, Philomene ambulanta, Philomene je ošetřovna, Philomene է հիվանդանոց, Philomene en erizaindegira, Philomene в лазарета, Philomene Krankenstation, Philomene* की दुर्बलता, *Philomene* の診療所, *Philomene ιατρείο του, Philomene ir lazarete, Enfermería de Philomene . . .*

Why she hadn't tried Spanish earlier? It brought her directly to a website Mersey Marsh would have loved: hospitalprofunda.com. It was all about a mythical subterranean hospital named Enfermería de Philomene that treated only supernatural creatures. The place was unique, and if you happened to be a fairy with a broken wing, or a Daredevil who'd come down with chicken pox, or a poltergeist who was hearing voices in its head, or Odin out with hammer-toe, then you were obliged to go to the Enfermería de Philomene, the only place in the world where treatment was available.

Humans, reported the website in twenty-four-point type dripping with blood, were not welcome.

Pauline harrumphed. She felt like she was reading one of Chance's dumb fantastical comic books.

The website's owner, Mateo Peña, a ham radio operator from Rincón Oscuro, Texas, a small town at the edge of Big Bend National Park, claimed to live directly above the hospital and occasionally intercept radio signals from the place. There was even a channel on the website, but there was nothing but static now.

Pauline hunted for a *contact* link on the website so she could write to Mateo, but there was none. Infuriating. She scoured the website instead. There was a vast amount of information. Most compelling was the infirmary's mail delivery system—a worldwide network of large underground pipes. Had Chance, by chance, broken into one at the bottom of his hole to China? And was he now stuck inside one of these pipes?

Pauline ran outside and climbed into the hole. Chills seized her at the sight of the chipped and broken pipe.

"Chance!"

Nothing. She climbed out of the hole, ran inside and past Pye, dozing on the couch, and bounded upstairs.

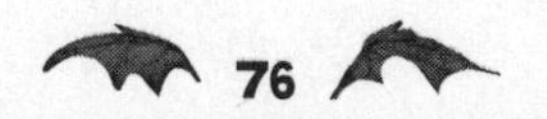

She wrote an e-mail.

> Dear Mersey,
>
> Chance is missing. I'm in a giant pipe at the bottom of the hole Chance dug. I think he's in the pipe. I'm going after him. Don't come after me. Don't let anyone know. Call over here and tell Pye (he's babysitting) I'm sleeping at your house. And if I'm not back, do it again the next night, and the next. Go to hospitalprofunda.com. It will tell you everything.
>
> I miss you.
>
> Love,
> Pauline

She loaded her pockets with supplies—mini flashlight, phone, batteries, peppermint candies, twenty bucks, and a pocketknife. She began to put on her sneakers, but there was something in the toe of the left shoe. Pauline stuck her hand in and withdrew an object not unlike a pretzel stick.

The missing piece of fulgurite.

She tucked it into a jeans pocket and ran downstairs.

She woke up Pye and told him she was spending the night at a friend's house. He grunted once, twice, and rolled over.

And Pauline was off.

CHAPTER 15

Chance looked out the elevator doors of the 1,290th floor of Saint Philomene's Infirmary for Magical Creatures onto a polished white hallway that was just like a regular hospital's. Across from him was what resembled a nurses' station; it was, however, free of nurses. He peeked around the corner. Empty, in both directions. The hallway seemed to go on infinitely. Along both sides were closed doors, each of which was numbered: 1290.344, 1290.345, and so on. In front of many doorways, monitors stood beeping and chiming. Chance gingerly stepped into the hallway. Not a soul. He ducked behind the nurses' station.

Computers!

Chance dragged a wheeled chair over and sat in front of a monitor. He could barely fit between the armrests. The monitor and keyboard were also small—he had to use the tip of his pocketknife to type. He studied the screen. Ah, there: site search. Chance typed in *infirmary directory*, then *Fallor Medoby Dox. No results found.* He tried just *Fallor.* Nothing. Chance took out his letter and read it again.

Aha.

Alas, there is not nearly enough to save 1,800,000 beings, my dear Simon, but, in your hands, it could save the one capable of saving the all.

Chance typed in *Simon*, which resulted in 5 hits:

—Simon Certainpants (Pixie)

staff, *anesthesiologist*, geriatrics, room 3299.124

—Crash Simons (Vampire)

staff, *bass player*, phlebotomists' lounge orchestra, room 2460.981

—Simone Uiough (Revenant)

staff, *lunch lady*, cafeteria 4449, meat line

—Simonetta Treathm-Popthm (Harrow-Teaguer)

staff, *Keeper of Perishable Organs*, rooms 800.100–800.110

—Simon Sleight (Deviklopt)

patient, *detainee*, (treachery), cell #299, basement

That last one. Chance remembered the number 299 from the envelope.

That's whom Chance was delivering the letter to.

Maybe this would all work out, and Chance could be home in time for lunch! Or dinner? He had lost track of time.

Except Saint Philomene's Infirmary for Magical Creatures appeared to be at least 4,449 floors deep, and who knew how much farther down the basement was. And he happened to be going to meet a prisoner. A Deviklopt, whatever that was. It certainly didn't sound like a being he wanted to spend much time with. It also sounded like he might be untrustworthy. But someone, Fallor Medoby Dox, whose very name comported loyalty, trusted Simon Sleight enough to place the welfare of everyone in the infirmary in his hands.

Chance returned to the site search and typed in *basement directions.*

Before the results registered, a loudspeaker blared and Chance fell out of his chair, landing hard on the white linoleum floor.

Attention.

Footsteps. Multiple footsteps, as though of a giant galloping centipede in jodhpurs. Getting closer. Chance ducked

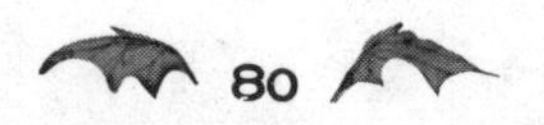

under the counter and crouched as far back as he could, among the computers' wires and cables and power strips.

> ***Attention: Perimeter breach, human, male, location floors 1,509 to 1,212, repeat: human, danger of infection, invoke all caution.***

Infection? Chance gulped. It felt like there was a lemon in his chest.

Chance tried to bury himself deeper among the wires and cables. The footsteps thundered louder.

"Check every room!" something shouted. "Look under every sheet, in every closet, behind every monitor, up every air duct!"

Affirmative shrieks and yells sounded as the footsteps scattered down the halls. What were they? They didn't sound like Balliopes. So far they hadn't thought to look behind the nurses' station. . . .

Suddenly, the overpowering fetor of boiled broccoli filled the room, and a brown patent-leather boot came into view. Then, a pair. And another pair, but these were in pink patent leather. From the tops of the boots emerged skinny but thickly furred legs—the same species as the ones in the mail room. Their legs were so close that Chance could have, if he had wished to, reached out and left a fingerprint on the shiny footwear. But he did not wish to do that.

The lemon in Chance's chest began to climb up his

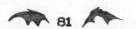

gullet. *This is impossible.* He was shaking so hard he worried they would hear his bones rattle.

"He's a slippery little human, huh, Kevin," said a being, the owner of the pink boots before him. He sounded a little like Moe from *The Simpsons*.

"We just started looking, Dan, jeez," said his companion, Kevin, in the brown boots.

"Lemme see the picture of him again," said the something called Dan.

Chance heard paper being unfolded. Chance was tired of the sounds paper could make.

"Ew, his ears stick way out."

Hey!

"And so dirty," added Dan.

"What the heck do you know, Dan? You've probably never seen a human in your life. For all you know, they *all* look like that."

"Not true. I did see one, for your information," said Dan, stamping one pink boot in indignation. "Remember that old human lady, decades ago? I helped catch her. I was lucky I didn't get infected with that horrible Oppaboffian bug she was carrying."

Chance thought he might faint. If they just happened to glance under the counter . . .

"Darn right. Killed a bunch of creatures in Donbaloh, that bug. Forget what it was called."

"How does one get to Oppabof, anyway?"

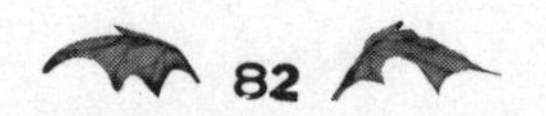

"Why? You wanna go live with the humans? Catch that bug you missed the first time?"

"Just curious, Kevin. Jeepers, don't bite my head off. Besides, plenty of nonhumans live on the surface. Sowlths, barrow-wights, kelpies, vampires—"

"Okay, okay. Well, first you have to get a bunch of shots. Then you have to apply for a visa from the Office of Transportation—"

"No, I mean, like, *secretly*, you know, through tunnels and whatnot."

"You're kind of freaking me out," said Kevin. "You know, if you leave, they'll never let you back in again. Especially Vyrndeets like ourselves."

"I'm just curious!"

"Fine," said Kevin, leaping up to sit on the counter directly over Chance, his brown-booted legs swinging forward and backward, the heels rising only inches from Chance's nose. "A map exists."

"A map! Where?"

"I dunno, but I've heard it's been circulating around Saint Philomene's in a manuscript for centuries. It must still be around because folks do occasionally, illegally, venture up to Oppabof, outside the proper channels. You'd have to talk to Arbipift Obriirpt, who is, officially, a personal bodyguard to Feargus M'Quiminy—"

"The Chief of Surgery?"

"Yep," said Kevin, pausing in his boot swinging. "But

Obriirpt is also, *un*officially, the guy that runs Saint Philomene's black market in transplant organs."

"What is he?"

"M'Quiminy and Obriirpt are both Harrow-Teaguers."

"Gad!" said Dan, crossing his pink boots.

"'Gad!' is about right, my friend. Either one of them could pinch your head off with two phalanges. Anyway, if anyone knows were the map is, it's him."

Arbipift Obriirpt. Arbipift Obriirpt. Arbipift Obriirpt. Chance said the name over and over in his head so he wouldn't forget it. Arbipift Obriirpt would be his ticket out of here.

A voice, neither Dan's nor Kevin's, shouted, "Floor clear!"

Dan and Kevin marched off. All was silent except the chirpy songs of the monitors. Chance emerged from under the nurses' station counter, stood up to stretch his cramped body, and peeked out into the hallway, where a Balliope sprayed him in the face with an aerosol that instantly blinded and nauseated him. Chance fell to the floor.

"Hah!" said the thing, whose voice sounded like a seal playing a harmonica. "You can elude a dull-witted Vyrndeet, but not a devious Balliope like *moi*! Ha-ha-ha!"

Chance—sightless, sick, supine—lost consciousness.

CHAPTER 16

When Josh Ringle called Mersey Marsh and asked her out on a date, she thought, *How much more promising could a summer day get?* But two nights later, Mersey found herself Josh-less, with an e-mail from her best friend announcing that she was chasing her brother down a subterranean pipe, perhaps never to return.

During the barbecue, Mersey had been unable to think of anything but Josh and what she could wear to make him fall in love with her, and she had spent most of the event up in her bedroom experimenting with different ensembles. Mersey's love fog obscured thoughts of anything else—pork ribs, corn on the cob, Uncle Dob and his weird wicker puppets, and, unfortunately, her friend Pauline Jeopard, whom Mersey could see from her bedroom window, sitting by herself at a crooked picnic table, eating chicken and waving away flies. Mersey was sure her friend understood how important this was to her. Mersey would go to Pauline's after the date the next night to tell her all about it.

Mersey Marsh decided on a black skirt and a black T-shirt illustrated with a tombstone reading RIP MERSEY MARSH. It had been a gift from her second-best friend, Lila Hammerglitz.

Mersey spent an hour shaping her brows into perfect arches and another hour on her face, a tour de force of painterly maquillage in lights and darks.

Josh had picked up Mersey on the corner a few houses down in an old olive-green pickup magnificently cratered with dents. He gave her a fake black rose.

"I couldn't find any real ones," he said with the merest hint of a lisp, which Mersey found thrilling.

"That's okay," she said. "I like fake flowers."

At the theater, Mersey sat, paralyzed by uncertainty over movie-date protocol, throughout *Buzzard People*, a cinematic failure about a chicken-borne virus that transformed infected humans into flightless birds of prey who feed on their uninfected brethren. When the movie was over, she had trouble bending her knees and elbows to stand up.

They went to Dairy Queen after, where Mersey continued her social paralysis. Josh appeared to have had some experience dating—he talked animatedly to Mersey about school, summer, Dr. Kinfiggish, his truck, and his passion for geology. Mersey smiled and nodded but added nothing.

They drove around town in his truck, drinking Dr Peppers. Slowly, Mersey became more comfortable. It got later and later. She was finally able to talk without stuttering, and she was able to glance over at Josh and admire his curly hair without worrying he would catch her.

During a conversation about national parks, Mersey glanced at her phone and noticed it was past one in the morning. She was supposed to be at Pauline's!

But Mersey did not want the date to end. Neither, apparently, did Josh, who continued to drive around, stopping for gas and more Dr Pepper, until four in the morning, when he finally stopped at the corner where he'd picked Mersey up. Mersey went home and slept until three in the afternoon. When she woke, she immediately called Josh.

"I really had fun, Josh . . . ," said Mersey.

"Look, I had fun and all, too, but, you know, I . . . but, well, I received a call today."

"A call? What do you mean?"

"A phone call. From someone."

Who? Mersey could not say it.

"From this person. In Mr. Fwope's algebra class. She . . ."

She. Mersey put her hand to her throat.

". . . wants to be my girlfriend."

Mersey missed Pauline so much at that moment she

could taste it, a bitter carbolic tang at the back of her tongue. All at once she felt horrible about neglecting her. She felt even worse for not considering how Pauline must be feeling about the date.

Who?

"Clarissa Speen," he said with what sounded like veiled triumph.

"Oh."

"She's, like, bugging me to go out with her. So."

Mersey felt faint. If she hadn't already been sitting down . . .

"That's cool," said Mersey. "Clarissa's cool."

"Well, uh," said Josh, "see you around?"

"Huh," said Mersey. "I do not think so."

Mersey hung up.

Mersey dialed Pauline. She was desperate to apologize to her friend for being so late, to explain. To cry on her shoulder, possibly. Yes.

But there was no answer.

Mersey checked her Gmail. She had four new messages.

The one from Pauline would change her life forever.

CHAPTER 17

Pauline hung helplessly in midair by the back belt loop of her jeans, which was hooked on a shiny steel talon of a great metal claw hanging from the arm of a crane in a vast room filled with mail, while three terrifying pig-turtle things with candy hats pointed at her. They appeared to be laughing, judging by the way they held their furry bellies and rocked on their heels, their pig-turtle mouths gaping wide.

Had Chance experienced this? Pauline didn't know if her brother could handle this sort of thing. Pauline wasn't sure if *she* could. Those creatures couldn't possibly be real—some kind of twisted robotics genius must have devised them. But some part of Pauline—the part that was scared of closed closets, stick insects, drains—*knew* those creatures were real. And this giant metal claw was certainly no illusion.

A huge drawer opened in one of the walls, as if a giant had pulled it out of a monumental dresser. The crane began to swing around, eventually poising itself directly over the open drawer. Without warning, the claw let go of Pauline, and she dropped into the drawer, which was actually a chute of some kind: a long, steep steel slide that, after a terrifying ride, deposited her like a gumball on the carpeted floor of a large, tidy room dominated by an oversize table surrounded by four oversize chairs. In one corner was a huge coffeemaker, in another, a gigantic filing cabinet. And in the middle of a wall was a fifteen-foot-tall door, its softball-sized doorknob too high for Pauline to reach. Pauline wondered if she'd somehow shrunk by half, or if everything really was double scale. Or if she was dreaming. Was she in bed at home, Chance in the next room, snoring like a pennywhistle? Of course. Only in a dream could such insanity unfold.

On the other side of the door, in the distance, there were whoops and yells and gleeful snorts, coming closer and closer.

They sounded very real. Maybe it wasn't a dream.

Humans are not welcome here, hospitalprofunda.com had said.

There was nowhere to hide. What would they do to

her? Put her in a pipe back to the surface, put her in a pen, put her in a pan, put her in quarantine, put her to death?

Pauline tried to open the bottom drawer of the filing cabinet, but it was locked.

If only she weren't human.

Pauline paused. *Hmm.*

She began to hunt through her pockets. Where were they? Had she lost them in the pipe, in the mail room, on the slide? The hoots and screams were getting closer. And now they were just on the other side of the door. A key rattled. . . .

Here they are! Right in her front pocket, way at the bottom. She popped one of Mersey's fangs on one tooth and the second on another just as the room began to swarm with creatures that looked like large leather beach balls. They were each wielding a medieval-looking halberd, some of whose tips appeared to be covered in blood. Pauline screamed.

"Hey," said one of the creatures, its voice high but waterlogged, like a baby gargling syrup. "She's not a human. Look, she's a vampiress."

"False alarm!" shouted one of the creatures, which Pauline later learned were called Balliopes and not considered very bright. "Everybody back to their stations!"

Most of the Balliopes left, disappointed their quarry wasn't one they could lance to death with medieval cutlery, but two remained behind with Pauline.

"Sorry to scare you, miss," said one of them, shutting the door behind him. "You won't bite me, will you?"

The Balliopes began to chuckle, a horrible sound, like drowning wildebeests.

"Seriously, are you all right? How did you get caught in a mail pipe?"

"I . . . I thought it was a, you know, a different pipe."

"Ah. Happens sometimes. Why are you here?"

"I have . . . uh, chicken pox."

Both the Balliopes stepped back a few paces.

"Whoa, I didn't even know vampiresses could get chicken pox."

"We can," said Pauline, praying the fangs wouldn't pop off while she was talking. "Can you tell me where to go?"

"Sure. Want a cup of coffee first?"

"Uh, no, it makes my fangs brown."

Both creatures nodded thoughtfully.

"Just follow us."

The Balliopes opened the giant door and led Pauline down a long blue hallway lined with doors and windows of different shapes and sizes until they came to a bank of elevators. More than a dozen sets of double doors, above each a sign indicating which floor it went to. Apparently they were on the 1,515th floor. One of the creatures pressed the UP button on an elevator that went up to the 1,456th.

"How many floors are there?" said Pauline, feeling somehow at ease with these creatures.

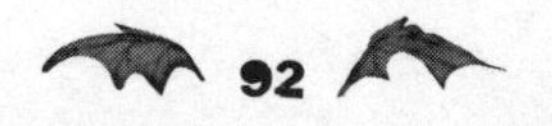

"Oh, around 6,250, though there are rumors of catacombs beneath the basement. All told, Saint Philomene's Infirmary for Magical Creatures is nearly ten miles deep. Plus, every floor is half a mile wide, half a mile long. Way down at the bottom are empty floors, broken elevators, junk, garbage, leaks, bad smells, corpses, armored mantle rats. Nobody goes down there. Except prisoners. That's where you would've gone if you'd been a human."

The Balliopes laughed.

One of the elevators had only a DOWN button. The sign above it read BASEMENT. A hand-lettered sign taped to the doors said BUSTED DON'T USE. If Chance had been captured, that's where he would be: the basement. It was worth a shot. Pauline surreptitiously leaned on the button to the broken basement-bound elevator while they were waiting for the elevator to the 1,456th floor. It seemed to take forever. Finally, their elevator door opened. At the same time, the door to the basement elevator opened. Pauline pretended to follow the two Balliopes onto their elevator, but just as the door was closing, she darted out and ran to the open basement elevator, realizing too late that the elevator car itself was not there. It was just an open shaft.

Pauline fell in.

She screamed for a full thirty seconds, tumbling in space, falling, falling, watching the numbered floors pass by her more and more quickly—1,810, 1,820, 1,830. Faster now, the air rushing by her at a 120 miles per hour—2,320, 2,330,

2,340. Calculating she had about two and a half minutes to live—3,190, 3,200, 3,210—oh, how she missed her mother and dad and brother. . . . Poor Chance, he would die alone at the bottom of Saint Philomene's Infirmary for Magical Creatures, just as it appeared she would, too—3,990, 4,000, 4,010—it was getting hard to breathe now, and her blood felt like it was boiling in her veins. Then, she drifted too close to a wall, hit it, the friction causing her to spin head over heels, now no longer able to read the floors as she fell, until she was able to right herself again—6,050, 6,060, 6,070—oh no, it was nearly over, less than half a mile to go. Pauline squinted into the depths, detached now from her fate, wondering with curiosity exactly what she would hit—6,090, 6,100, 6,110—wait, what was that below, at the bottom? It was brown, jagged in a way, coming closer—6,190, 6,200, 6,210 . . . what?

Boxes?

Pauline was suddenly in a world of cardboard. When she finally came to rest, she had compressed forty feet of empty boxes into ten. She slowly made her way up through all the crushed boxes that had closed around her as she fell through them, found the doors to the 6,249th floor, pried them open with her hands, and climbed onto a darkened, abandoned hallway. Right next to the elevator was a door marked STAIRS. She opened it, climbed down one flight, then opened another door, put an empty tin can between it and the jamb so it wouldn't lock behind her, and found herself in the basement,

directly across from Cell #1, which contained, of all things, a Balliope. It appeared to be dead. Cell #2 was empty, as were numbers 3 and 4. But Cell #5 housed a creature that an instant's inspection revealed to be a true vampire, who came at her with such speed and bloodthirstiness that Pauline thought it would break the thick bars containing it.

"You are a fraud," the vampire said, its voice shrill and cold, its malarial eyes seeming to bore right through her. "Come closer, let me pluck out those fictions!"

Pauline hurried away, the vampire screaming as she jogged along the dark, endless hallway, illuminated by small pitch torches in sconces on the passageway walls. Each torch provided the only light to the cells, which were either empty or domiciled by bizarre creatures, all of whom were in one of two states: active (leaping, crashing, screeching, thrusting, writhing) or inactive (deceased or sleeping or catatonic or simply unwilling to move). The odor was such that Pauline had never experienced. Every imaginable fetor and musk, the top note of which was the smell of sweaty feet, assaulted her olfactory nerves and stung her eyes.

"Chance!" she shouted, jogging by the cells, one by one. "Chance, are you here?"

She stopped. She looked around.

This is ridiculous. This is not happening. The evidence of her senses now contradicted everything she thought she knew to be the steep truths of the world. So she was simply *off.* Maybe she'd eaten some bad Count Chocula. Or maybe she'd gone psychotic with worry about her brother. She was sure she'd come to her senses and all this would be a figment, a memory.

To prove this to herself, Pauline, the devout skeptic, wound up and punched the "stone wall." Hard.

"Ow!"

Maybe the "stone wall" was in fact a stone wall, without the quotes. Hm. Maybe it would be in her best interests to accept, for now, this manifest world.

She walked down the corridor. She stopped in front of a cell divided into twenty-four tiny cages, none larger than a cat carrier, each containing a very small being; some were vicious, snarly monsters worrying the bars of their cages with dull, broken teeth; others were beatific, comely things blinking their gorgeous eyelashes at her; still others Pauline recognized to be, without a doubt in the world, gnomes.

"Help us!" they said, thrusting their tiny hands through the bars, reaching for Pauline.

She looked up. Cells #120, 121, 122. How many cells were there? A quarter of a square mile's worth? She hurried on through the murk and stink, closing her ears to screams; dodging outstretched arms and tentacles and other articulated protuberances; ducking torrents of spit issued by members of a fishlike species who must have been innately bad or recidivistic, given the disproportionate number populating the cells.

"Chance!"

Some creature in a cell way down the passageway nasally mimicked her voice. "Cha-a-a-nce!"

Finally, at Cell #299, she stopped. She took out her envelope again, shining her little flashlight on it. Resident 251987. Yes, Cell #299.

"Chance?"

No movement.

In a far corner, on a crude mattress at the base of a rough stone wall blackened by time and filth, lay a shortish elf-like figure that was on his back, eyes open, mouth wide, clawed hands frozen, grasping at air, a long thick chain next to him.

"Sir?"

The creature did not move. Pauline pitched a small stone at it, which pinged off its forehead. No response. She was about to throw another when she noticed its mouth move.

The mouth, inexplicably, opened wider. A huge white tongue began to protrude.

"Sir!"

Except it wasn't a tongue. It was a worm.

Pauline screamed and fell back against the cell behind her. She finally settled herself, stood up, and shined her flashlight on the worm. She shuddered and was about to move on when she noticed something on the rear wall. She moved up to the bars and peered in, her flashlight focused on a drawing.

A bee.

Chance was alive!

Chance used to draw bees all the time. On account of his middle name: Bee.

They must have caught him and put him in here. How did he get out? Was he taken out, maybe by a judiciary that planned to interrogate him? Or did he escape? And if the latter, where could he possibly have gone?

Think, Pauline, think! Where would I go if I were Chance? Maybe he had sought out the dead elf-like thing in the cell in order to deliver the letter that had been in the envelope now in her possession. Maybe the being had told him where to go. But where could that be? Maybe Chance, succeeding in his mission, had endeavored to find his way home?

Pauline noticed one of the cell's badly corroded bars was broken, allowing enough space for a boy of Chance's dimensions to squeeze through. That he had broken it did not surprise her; Chance could be creatively ingenious. Perhaps he was already home. If only she could make a call or send an e-mail or something, but her phone didn't work down here at all.

How to proceed? Pauline sat down in the filthy passageway and put her head in her hands. A headache was starting, possibly from the air pressure at such a great depth, not to mention the voices in her head.

What does she think she's doing there? said a voice in her skull, as if on cue.

Pauline shook her head to rid herself of the voices, but it

did no good. They kept on, assaulting her like a straight-line wind.

Oh, where is she?

The voice actually sounded familiar. Was Pauline going crazy? She had read about the harrowing trials of insanity, the profound ways in which people afflicted with off-balance brain chemistry could suffer. It would explain everything she'd seen. Or *thought* she had seen. Was everything a hallucination?

She'd better make it back home.

Is this what it was like? A stream of words she couldn't turn off?

She's going to die there.

"Shut up!" Pauline screamed.

Oh! Someone just screamed "shut up" in my head! said the voice.

What? Maybe Pauline truly was going crazy. Now the voice was hearing voices in *its* head.

This would never have happened if I hadn't been so selfish, said the voice.

Pauline banged her head on the hard stone floor, but it didn't help.

"I need you, Mersey!" shouted Pauline as loudly as she could, but the thick, fetid air and dank walls and utter darkness swallowed it up.

What? said the voice.

"What?"

I said, What?

"I said I need Mersey."

Pauline was sure she'd lost it; she was now conversing with the voice in her head.

I need you, too. Uh, where are you?

Ah, the voice sounded like Mersey.

"I refuse to answer a nonexistent entity!" shouted Pauline.

Pauline's voice is in my head. Am I going nuts?

"Uh, Mersey?"

Pauline?

"That couldn't possibly be you, could it?"

And that couldn't possibly be you, could it?

"I can't see how. Yet it appears to be true. Oh my, I've lost my mind."

Pauline, said the Mersey figment in her head, *you wouldn't happen to be in possession of the missing piece of fulgurite?*

"What are you talking about?"

Do you have it or not?

"I . . . do."

That's how we're communicating. Remember what the internet said? Two pieces from the same fulgurite can allow long-distance communication?

At first Pauline refused to believe this. It just wasn't possible.

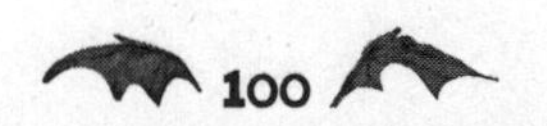

On the other hand . . . pig-turtles shouldn't have been possible, either. Or vampires. Or Balliopes. Or vast underground hospitals devoted to keeping them hale.

"I . . . I guess so," said Pauline, allowing herself to believe, the relief she was not alone so potent she was forced to put her head between her knees to keep from fainting. "Mersey, you won't believe this, but I'm in the basement of a ten-mile-deep hospital."

I know; I'm on the website—unbelievable.

"I can't find Chance; he was here, in a jail cell, but he's escaped, and I have no idea where to find him."

Don't worry. I will help. You're not alone.

CHAPTER 18

Chance woke to find himself in a round room with yellow walls, secured to a low table with thick woven straps like seat belts. His eyes were burning from whatever chemical he'd been sprayed with, his sinuses felt stuffed with rubber bullets, his tongue was swollen to twice its size, and his throat was virtually closed off. He coughed. A Balliope stood and made its way over.

"What's the matter, little human?" it said. It was wearing a surgical mask.

"Everything hurts."

The Balliope nearly fell to pieces laughing.

"Whoo!" it said. "Priceless! Well, just so you know, you won't feel much better where you're going."

"Where?" Chance felt he had nothing to lose by being direct.

"The basement, baby. The jail."

"No!"

Chance's pockets felt light. They had probably taken everything. Had they found the letter, too?

"Yes. The jail. Ha-ha-ha!"

"Please, at least don't put me in cell number two hundred ninety-nine!"

The Balliope looked at him closely. Chance noticed it was wearing a name tag: Nurtzi-Clajk.

"You," said Nurtzi-Clajk, "have absolutely no say over which cell you get. *Pal.*"

"Anywhere but number two hundred ninety-nine, have mercy!" said Chance, pretending to cry. Or was he pretending? He couldn't tell. He felt pretty awful, and he thought a real cry might do him good.

The door opened and four more Balliopes strode in, their long halberds nearly poking the ceiling. Each was wearing a gas mask. Did they think he was infectious?

"Finally," said Nurtzi-Clajk. "What took so long? Never mind. Chet, take our human to the basement."

"Where?" said Chet, the largest Balliope.

"Why," said Nurtzi-Clajk, "Cell number two hundred ninety-nine, of course."

"Nooo!" wailed Chance, delighted. Reverse psychology never worked on his sister.

Chet wheeled him into yet another hallway, this one beige and green. Unlike the last hallway he'd been in, it was bustling with all sorts of beings. Some were in wheelchairs, slowly rolling down the hall, weaving among the hurrying figures of creatures dressed in hospital scrubs, who in turn dodged creatures wheeling mops and buckets and pushing laundry hampers and carrying bags of mail. Everyone dodged the golf carts hurtling down the hall, their drivers yelling *"Delivery for Miss Tolphrinombah"* or *"Emergency, coming through,"* or *"Looking for Mr. Phlees Irkis."* The whole scene, in spite of its frantic pace, seemed perfectly choreographed.

Chet took elevator after elevator after elevator, embarking and disembarking, sometimes even backtracking, and, several times, taking trams from one bank of elevators to another on the same floor; hours and hours of this went by until a rickety elevator made entirely of wood dropped them off at the basement.

"Gah, I forgot how much it stinks down here," said Chet, locking the door to the elevator. He started down the hall, jabbing at all the creatures that were reaching out of their cages for him. "Back, vermin, back!"

They slowly made their way along the dark passageway, lit only by pitch torches every dozen yards, until they reached Cell #299.

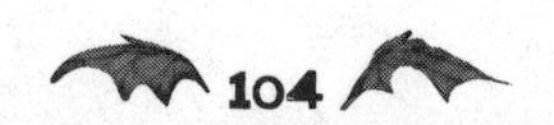

"Hey," said Chet. "There's already some dude in here. Hey, buddy, wake up, you got a roommate!"

The cell was indeed the domicile of a short elf-like man shackled to the wall by a long chain attached to his ankle. His long, stringy hair hung in greasy clumps. Very greasy, as though dipped in lard. Gross. Chet unstrapped Chance, dragged him in, and locked the door behind him with a many-toothed key. The being hissed at him with a deranged look, his greasy locks flying about his head. Chance cowered in a corner as far away as possible from Simon Sleight, if this was in fact he.

"Human, I don't want to ever see you again," said Chet, in a way that seemed to prophesy an encounter in the not-too-distant future.

Chance waited until Chet was out of sight, then checked his pocket. *Ah, thank heavens.* The letter was still there. All he had to do was deliver it, get out of this infernal cell, find Arbipift Obriirpt and the escape map, and flee.

"Hello," said Chance.

"Fie!" shouted the thing, slowly getting to its feet.

Chance said, "Are you, uh, Si—"

"*May* it please the gods dawdling in their pantheon above, what in the name of Donbaloh have I done to warrant the close and fetid society of a *human* companion? Are you colonized with disease? Not that it matters to me."

"I—"

"When," it said, its voice rising, "in the infinite curve of time has a *détenu* of the sacred bowels of the great infirmary's terminal story been obliged to share a cell with another being of *any* ilk?"

"—have a note—"

"And a child, no less—a gobbling, stupefied tween—innocent of all suffering, devoid of reason and a past, and delivered, I suppose, by the same vengeful bureaucracy that deposited me into this reeking Hades to begin with!"

"—from—"

"O, why must I suffer not only the chary gruel and botulinal water so infrequently imparted me, but also the obligation to share it with what is clearly a ravenous beastie of bottomless gut?"

"—Fallor—"

"Whom I cannot dispatch in my shoe box duchy—for who would remove its corpse?—and whom I cannot flog into silence, as the strength I once possessed in such abundance has now been withered by Iptid's Misery, which will at any moment render me deceased!"

"—Medoby—"

"Nor whom can I disregard: Who among the living can allow a mosquito to suck its very ichor without slapping it away or permit the mantle rat to gnaw at one's feet without punting it into space?"

"—Dox—"

"And, furthermore, why does a spineless piglet . . . Just a moment here. *What* did you say, human?"

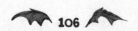

"What?"

"Were you just invoking the name Fallor Medoby Dox?" said Detainee 251987.

"Uh, yes," said Chance, more than a little frightened of this thing even though it appeared to be in ill health, presumably from Iptid's Misery, whatever that was. "I'm here to deliver a letter from him."

"To me?"

"Maybe," said Chance. "What's your name?"

"Simon. Simon Sleight, Deviklopt, thank you very much."

Chance removed the soiled and multiply creased letter from his back pocket and handed it to Simon, who snatched it away with one hand, crawled over to the bars, and read it in the dim light of a torch.

"Human, how did you come to be in possession of this?"

Chance told him.

"And . . . and you risked your own life to save a population you were not even sure was extant?"

"Uh, I guess, uh, I felt really bad taking the letter in the first place."

"Yes, that was without a doubt a reprehensible act of impropriety. However, I must admit that the chances of my receiving this letter through the customary channels were very slim indeed—postal delivery is, to say the least, not very reliable here in Saint Philomene's, and it's quite absent on the penal floors. Your bringing it personally speaks well not only of you, but of the human race."

"Oh, well—"

"Prithee, what is your name and title?"

"Chance. Uh, *kid*."

"Kid Chance."

"Just *Chance* is fine."

"*Chance* it is then," said the Deviklopt, carefully placing the unfolded letter on the floor. "Chance, I have much to ask of you."

"What?" said Chance, looking around the cell. As old and decrepit as it was, it still appeared sturdy enough to retain a boy and a fever-wracked Deviklopt forever.

"The one million eight hundred thousand patients and staff members of Saint Philomene's Infirmary for Magical Creatures are, unknowingly, at the mercy of a vile madman, a lone evildoer, a desperate and self-serving criminal who happens to have little time left on this side of the meager scrim separating life from death. Perhaps less than a day or two."

Simon began to cough—breathless, rib-shaking, spasmodic hacks that alarmed Chance.

"Simon!"

"It's all right, all is well," he said, the fit finally subsiding. "As you may have surmised, I am not well, either. I will also be gone soon, likely in less than twenty-four hours."

"But the paper," said Chance. "The flerk. We can save you."

"Indeed."

Simon produced a tin can from somewhere. He picked

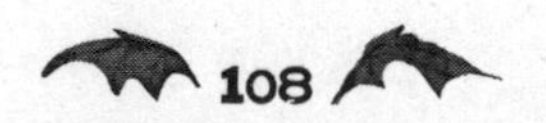

up the letter and wadded it up into a small ball, then placed it in the can. From a tin bucket he poured in just enough water to cover the paper ball, then set it on the ground.

"Two hours we wait. Have you a watch?"

"No, but I can count seconds without thinking about it." Chance did not want to know how Simon planned to spill twelve drops of his own blood.

"Then begin counting, young savant. Where was I? Ah! The sociopathic monster with our lives in its hands. You see, it is a human. Like yourself."

"How did it get in?" Chance felt strange calling a human an *it*, but when in Rome . . .

"In Oppabof—which I'm sure you've realized is our name for the terranean world you humans inhabit, along with vampires, kelpies, so on and so forth—there is a very rare disease. There it is called JENCKX30; here it is called GIGI. It is always fatal in Oppabof. Here in the infirmary, however, there exists a treatment."

"Is it flerk?" said Chance, wondering idly how Simon Sleight was planning to boil off the water when the time came.

Simon threw his head back and laughed.

"If only it were that easy. No, lad, flerk will not cure the madman. Only a certain medicine can do it. And there is only one creature that knows how to concoct that drug. And that creature, Yryssy Ayopy, a Geckasoft, is also very ill and has only a few days left to live, at most. She is in a deep

coma. But now that we will soon have a dose of precious flerk, it must be delivered to Yryssy so she may be cured and then able to deliver the medicine, called Ypocrasyne, to the human with GIGI: Dave Green, from Lubbock, Texas."

"Why is Yryssy the only one that knows how to concoct Ypocrasyne?"

"The formula was considered so sensitive that it was passed down only by word of mouth from Yryssy's grandfather, who developed it, to Yryssy's father, to Yryssy. Yryssy is the only survivor in the Ayopy line, so now she is the only one who knows it."

"Why is Dave Green so bad?"

"Dave Green is in control of a virus that he will release into the air, killing every last living thing in Saint Philomene's Infirmary for Magical Creatures, unless Yryssy is revived and cures him of GIGI. He will then return to Oppabof. But if he feels he will die, he will release the virus. He is quite mad. That is the issue—GIGI, in its end stages, drives one, er, as they say, bonkers."

"But how did he get here in the first place?"

Simon grew quiet. He peered into the tin can, swirled it about once or twice, and set it down.

"I play chess."

"Chess ?"

"Yes."

"Okay."

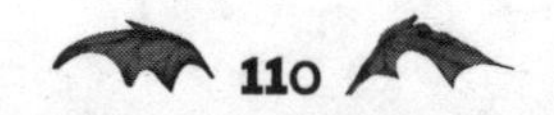

More silence. This was awkward. Chance was about to say "I do Pokémon" when Simon said, "I am a destructive force in the main line of the Ruy Lopez, and a concrete bunker with the Sicilian Defense, Najdorf Variation. Care for a game while we wait?"

"Uh, okay," said Chance, wondering where Simon kept his chessboard, whether there would be enough light to see, and why he wasn't answering his question.

"Very well. As I shall be dying soon, I will claim the privilege of white for the first game. Ready?"

"Uh . . ."

"Good," said Simon, closing his eyes. "e4."

Chance thought himself fairly adept at chess, especially when sacrificing pieces for positional advantages, but he was not sure if he could play without a chessboard. Or pieces. He had certainly never tried.

He closed his eyes, too, and pictured a white pawn on e4, the black array before him.

"e5."

"Nf3."

And Chance squeezed his eyes tight and essayed his imaginary c knight, the classic Ruy Lopez, an opening systematically studied in a 1561 book but known to have been included in the Göttingen manuscript in 1490. Simon attacked the knight with a bishop, Chance repelled it with a6, and the fight was on, but Chance knew that he was really

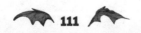

just playing the opening from memory—once he got to the fifteenth move he would be at sea. And that was exactly what happened. A few treacherous moves on Chance's part, and Simon played 21. c5! threatening c6, a discovered check. Chance thought for almost an hour, retreated a knight, then lost his mental image of the board and resigned before Simon could even play.

Simon opened his eyes.

"Well. You are a fine player, though I did not understand your bishop fianchetto at . . . 17! I suppose it is for the best that I accept your resignation. I would just be putting off answering your question about how Dave Green got here. So. Ever since I came to the infirmary—I was admitted for treatment of Iptid's Misery, of course, three weeks ago—I have not been able to find a suitably skilled opponent in-house, apart from Yryssy Ayopy, who works here at Saint Philomene's. She came to my room twice for a game, wearing a hazmat suit since Iptid's Misery is highly contagious (don't worry, humans are not at risk), but for the most part, she was too busy to play. So I found a computer terminal, hacked out of our infirmary intranet onto the Oppabof internet, and signed on to ChessKnight.com, which Yryssy is also a member of. This, as you can imagine, is verboten. After several games with talentless punters, I found an opponent a good deal better than I. Ultimately, I won seventeen and drew nineteen out of the sixty-seven games we played—and we started up a banter during games. I, of course, didn't reveal I was from Donbaloh—not even one in a million subterranean creatures would—but he did eventually tell me he was dying of an incurable disease."

"GIGI," said Chance.

"Yes. I had grown fond of him and valued him as an opponent. In a rash moment of empathy, I told him about Saint Philomene's Infirmary for Magical Creatures and Yryssy Ayopy, who was in possession of a cure."

"He believed you?"

"Not at first. But what did he have to lose? I informed him of a pipe entryway within the third Dumpster behind an Albertsons franchise in Lubbock. I told him to vault into the Dumpster at a certain instant and he'd suddenly find himself in a little cart in a large pipe, moving at about ninety-five miles per hour. But I advised him to disguise himself beforehand. I told him to shave his head and put on some Marilyn Manson contact lenses and pretend he's a ghoul, which is another race of Oppabof creatures that is susceptible to GIGI. Ghouls, unlike humans, are welcome here. Before long, Dave Green had arrived in Pipeport 311 and was being whisked to a private room to wait for Yryssy to concoct enough Ypocrasyne to cure him.

"But when they told Dave Green Yryssy was ill and unavailable to treat him, he lost his mind. He stormed through the hallways upsetting carts of surgical instruments, screaming, cursing out nurses and techs and maintenance crews, flinging insults, slamming doors, threatening ruin, tipping over creatures in sickbeds, and worse."

"Worse?"

"Indeed."

"Why didn't the Balliopes just come get him and put him in jail?"

"Dave Green, who is a biochemist working for the United States government, produced a small amber vial and brandished it before the Balliopes who had gathered around him. He said it was a biological warfare virus called Terabug. He warned the Balliopes that if he dashed the vial to the floor, the virus would disperse throughout the infirmary in a matter of hours and kill every creature in it. He said that if they didn't believe him, they should look him up on the internet—he was famous."

"That sounds outrageous," said Chance. "How could he expect a medical miracle to come from a death threat?"

"Well, as I mentioned before . . ."

"He's nuts. . . ."

"In fact and indeed."

"How do they know he really has a deadly virus?"

"They don't."

"But they can't risk that he's bluffing, I guess."

"Correct. And given his line of work, it is not impossible. He demanded to be put in contact with the chairman of the infirmary board, Sir Amk Bittius the Fourth, a Deviklopt;

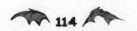

Mr. Green was given a two-way radio handset and submitted all his threats to him. The general population of the hospital had—has—no idea they're in danger. Only Bittius, the chief of staff, security (the Balliopes), and a few doctors know. And you and me. Dave Green said if he noticed any signs of an evacuation, he'd release the virus."

"How do you know all this?"

"When Bittius asked Dave Green how he got here, my chess name, sleight_of_hand, naturally came up, and they quickly found out who I was. So when those accursed Balliopes arrested me for treason and corruption of infirmary security, I pretended I was unconscious, and then overheard them talking.

"As we speak, Dave Green is wandering the halls and crevices and grottoes of Saint Philomene's Infirmary for Magical Creatures, probably still disguised as a ghoul, gripping his tube of Terabug—if, in fact, that is what it is—while the very best doctors in the entire hospital work around the clock trying to revive Yryssy Ayopy, to no avail. So far."

"Why is she so sick?"

Simon was silent again. He picked up the tin can again and looked inside.

"How much time left?" he said.

"It's been almost exactly two hours," said Chance.

"Good."

Simon sat up. He put the tin can in his lap; took out the waterlogged paper; squeezed the excess back into the can;

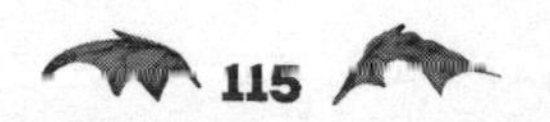

opened his mouth, revealing razorlike teeth; bit into the karate-chop edge of his right hand; let the blood run down his arm—or leg, depending on whether one considered him more human or more something else—then held his hand directly over the cup, counting the drops of blood as they splashed in the water.

". . . nine, ten, eleven, annnnd . . . twelve! That should do it. Now, my dear Chance, let us count two more hours."

Chance was getting anxious. Two more hours, then they somehow had to boil away most of the water—who knew how long that would take! Meanwhile, Yryssy Ayopy was dying, Dave Green was dying, Simon Sleight was dying, and Chance was locked up with no possible way of getting out. The flerk had to be delivered to Yryssy immediately, but there was no way to do so!

"To answer your question, Chance, Yryssy Ayopy has Iptid's Misery, just as I do. She caught it from me, in spite of the hazmat suit, when she visited to play chess. She has an acute form of it and will die within days. The demise of this infirmary, and the mass death of its inhabitants from Terabug infection, will be on my hands. Unless I can get this flerk to her. As soon as possible.

"Now, I must rest," he continued. "You must stay awake and count seconds. Wake me when the two hours are up. During that waiting period, I pray you will 1) hope none of the principal players die and 2) find a way out of here. You appear a clever fellow."

Simon fell back, his greasy hair spreading out on the mattress. He immediately began to snore. The cell was empty except for a zinc bowl for his food; his water bucket; a few candle stubs and some matches; the filthy mattress, which was made of a large, clear trash bag apparently stuffed with roots; a foot-long iron rod lying on the ground; and the long chain attached to his ankle. *What to do!* Chance paced and paced. Nothing came to him. He would die here.

Chance picked up the iron rod. It was a half-inch thick. He tried to pry open the bars of the cell, but there was no adequate fulcrum. The rod was useless, unless, perhaps, he could chip his way out through the stone. But that would take months. Chance put the rod down and continued to pace. He thought as hard as he could. He thought so hard his jaw hurt.

"Simon?"

"Present!" Simon shouted, bolting upright, eyes wide open. "Oh, er, is it time to get up?"

"It's been almost two hours."

"Certainly. Let me prepare a small fire with roots from my mattress. Where are my matches?"

"There."

"Ah."

Simon lit the first match, but it immediately fizzled out. The second caught, but the roots were too damp to catch.

"Give me your trousers, boy!"

Chance hesitated, but then took them off. He figured, *What the heck. How am I worse off in just my Undcroos?*

But Simon could not get the jeans lit, either. He was down to one match. He was about to light it when Chance said, "Wait!"

Chance pulled a few hairs out of his own head, then a few more, and a few more, until he had made a little nest of kindling on the ground.

"That'll burn," he said. "When it's lit, hold my jeans over it. They'll catch easier that way."

"Brilliant," said Simon, smiling, revealing his razorlike teeth.

Simon lit the last match. He cupped his hand around it, coaxing the flame, blowing gently, gently to feed it oxygen. Then he lit Chance's hair, which caught easily and burned rapidly. Simon held Chance's jeans over the flame.

But they didn't catch. The flames went out. Simon lay back on his root bag.

"We are doomed," he said. Simon began to moan in anguish.

"Stop that now," said Chance.

Chance stood and looked through the bars. Across the passageway was a sconce in the wall holding a pitch torch.

The torch was at least two feet out of his reach. He grabbed the end of one jeans leg, reached outside the bars, and using the jeans like a bullwhip, snapped at the torch, finally connecting after two dozen tries, knocking it out of its sconce and onto the passageway floor. With the jeans-whip, it was easy to drag the torch close enough to grab it.

"Bravo, young human," said Simon. "Now hand it to me."

Simon fashioned a small stove out of stones. The liquid started to boil. When it was reduced to a thimbleful, Simon removed it from the stove.

"Drink some," said Chance. "What're you waiting for? We have to save *you* before we can save Yryssy."

But Simon ignored him. Instead, he tore a small scrap of plastic from his trash-bag mattress. He pushed his thumb into the middle of the scrap so it stretched and made a deep indentation. Then he poured the flerk into it, plucked a thread out of his tunic, and used it to tie off the little plastic pouch.

"Here," he said, pressing the small flerk balloon into Chance's hand. "Geckasofts, just so you know, are delicate, slim gray creatures about three feet high, wrinkled, much like Oppaboffian elephants, with long snouts and large eyes. Yryssy is particularly slender. You must take this to her. You must get it into her mouth somehow, all of it, every drop."

"But . . . but . . . what about you?"

"There is only enough for one being."

"You mean . . ."

"Yes."

"I can't let you die!"

"We have no choice. Either I die alone or everyone dies."

Simon lay back on his mattress. His mouth opened. His hands reached up, clawing at the air, then appeared to freeze solid, midgrasp.

"Simon!"

"Get out of here, Kid Chance," he said so quietly that Chance had to bend over and put his ear near Simon's mouth. "Go."

"I can't leave you!"

"Perhaps," he said, closing his eyes, "but I am leaving you."

"Wait! Tell me where Yryssy is!"

Simon Sleight did not respond.

Chance touched his friend's throat; no pulse. Did Deviklopts even *have* pulses? Chance put Simon's wrist to his forehead. Simon's body seemed to be growing cool. Was he dead? Chance had never seen anything that big dead. Birds and armadillos and raccoons . . . and, well, that leathery skeleton on the 1,509th floor. But not Deviklopts. Chance stood up and screamed.

"Help! Help!"

But all he could hear was some creature in another cell far away mimicking him: *Hay-yulp! Hay-yulp!*

Chance rattled the bars of the cell, but they were absolutely solid. He put his pants back on, placed the precious balloon of flerk in his pocket. He lay down on the warm stone floor and quickly fell asleep.

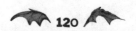

Chance awoke with a violent start, sweating, mouth completely dry. He looked around. Some creature had left a paper bowl of food and a tin of water. He drank the water, which tasted like iron. The food looked like a very large piece of jellyfish sushi. He nibbled at the slimy, slippery thing. It tasted like chicken. He ate quickly.

The torch, leaning against the wall, was running out of fuel; it burned only dimly now, the flame a thin gauze of blue. Simon had not moved; he lay still on his mattress, mouth open, clawing at nothing. Insects had found him, strange Donbaloh bugs, and were beginning to crawl on his face, up his wrists to his hands, over his manacled ankle.

The chain. Could Chance use it somehow? He crawled over to examine the manacle. He touched Simon's foot, which felt smooth, cool, and spongy. It didn't appear the manacle would easily come off over the foot, even though it was fairly thin and bony. Chance tried all the same. If only he had a shoehorn of sorts, or oil to use as a lubricant, he *might* be able to get it off. But there was nothing like that.

Chance stood, but nearly slipped when he trod on a lock of Simon's long, ultragreasy hair that had trailed onto the ground.

Ah.

Chance scooped up a palmful of Simon's extraordinarily copious hair grease, slathered it on the Deviklopt's chained ankle, and, with no little effort, slipped off the manacle.

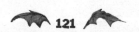

The chain was longer than the cell was deep, one end anchored to the wall. Chance tied the other end around a bar of the cell door, in the manner of a tightrope. He climbed up and stood on the chain, balancing by putting his hands on the ceiling. But his weight wasn't great enough; the bar didn't budge. He pushed on the ceiling as hard as he was able to, but no dice.

Chance jumped down. He glanced at Simon. Strange insects were all over him now, crawling in and out of his ears and mouth and nose. Chance shuddered and turned away, accidentally stepping on the iron rod and nearly falling again. He picked it up.

He stuck one end of the rod through a link in the middle of the chain stretched between the wall and the bar on the cell door. He turned the rod once, beginning to twist the chain. He turned it again. The chain began to tauten. Another turn, another, and another. The chain creaked and groaned, so high was the magnitude of its tension. Chance turned the rod again. It was becoming more and more difficult. What would give first? The chain, snapping at its weakest link; the wall, where the end of the chain was anchored; or Chance, himself, unable to turn the rod any farther?

Chance, with a low *grrr* of concentration and effort, turned it once more.

Bink! The chain snapped and smashed into the back wall. The rod had been stripped out of his hands, and Chance was knocked onto his back. He looked up at the cell door.

The bar had broken in half under the tension of the torquing chain, leaving enough room for Chance to squeeze through. Before he did so, however, he crawled around the floor, located the iron rod, and used it to scratch a design on the wall.

A bee.

He touched Simon on the arm, murmured, *"I won't fail you,"* tucked the iron rod in his belt, then squeezed through the bars of Cell #299, finally falling into the passageway, liberated.

He had to find Yryssy Ayopy. *Now.*

CHAPTER 19

What Pauline needed more than anything else right now was a destination.

"Mersey, where am I going?" she said.

I don't know, said Mersey, deep inside Pauline's head. *I'm trying to tune in to a signal to get some information—the appearance of a human down there would be big news, and it would be talked about on Infirmary Radio (WSPI). According to hospitalprofunda.com, I might be able to pick up a two-way radio down there, which the security forces use. But at the moment, all I can pick up is Muzak.*

"Mersey, you're fading."

Wh—?

"What?"

And Mersey was gone. Pauline supposed fulgurite transmitters were subject to communication blackouts, too, although in her circumstances, that could prove *very* inconvenient.

Where could Chance be? Probably staying out of sight, maybe traveling by air duct or little-used elevators and forgotten staircases. Pauline presumed he was trying to get out now, having delivered his letter to Simon Sleight. But how? Maybe Chance knew how. But if he didn't, he'd go to the top floor, wouldn't he? The one closest to the surface of the Earth? Yes. Then that's where she would go, too.

After an hour of running up and down rows of cells, she finally found an elevator, but it was locked and appeared to need three separate keys to open. There were no other elevators; all she could find was passageway after passageway of dank cells. Where were the jailers? *Someone must look after these beings!* Pauline decided it was not her business to worry about the beings in the cells. It was her business to find her brother, then get out of that hole and go home to her mother and her Mersey and continue on with life, right where they left off.

So Pauline found the door to the stairs she had used to enter the basement, and she began to climb, story after story, stealing out onto each floor to see if elevators could be found. This far down, the floors were simply abandoned,

tomblike expanses, each a finger deep in what looked like centuries of dust and decay, and some so dark and forbidding they gave Pauline chills. She hastily closed the doors on those places and continued her ascent.

Floor 6,199 was different. It was actually a seven-story room, entirely open, a quarter of a mile in area, filled from end to end and floor to ceiling with hundreds and hundreds of machines, their great shiny silver frameworks filled with bronze gears spinning at greater and lesser speeds, red-painted funnels atop every one, each spouting steam, and sealed ducts leading to the next floor high above, each looking like a huge metal cobra striking the ceiling. Every machine was manned by a creature of a different species, from tiny beasts that looked like mouse skeletons to four-story colossi resembling finless zebra-striped whales who were waving around dozens of long, thin, multijointed arms like daddy longlegs' legs. Each creature was pushing buttons or yanking levers or mopping its brow or scribbling on a yellow pad.

There were recognizable creatures, too—a tall, thin, corroded zombie with half a face, a bonafide werewolf, and what appeared to be Cinderella's fairy godmother. She was shorter than Pauline had always imagined.

Pauline ducked behind a little cart filled with flywheels and thick blue cables, peeking around every so often, trying to decide what to do. *Just walk up to one of them and ask for directions? Well, why not?*

She was about to take a deep breath, stand up, and stroll

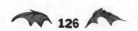

over to the fairy godmother when a creature that looked like a schnauzer-sized dung beetle in a leotard prodded Pauline on the rear end with a yardstick.

"Whatcha doin'?" it said, in a voice like a honking cat. "Looking for a neck to bite?"

"Well, no. I'm, uh, staying on the chicken pox floor, and I decided to go for a little walk, and, you know, got lost."

That's my story, and I'm sticking to it.

"Well," it said, stepping back. "You can't be on the Climate Floor. This is where all the air-conditioning comes from, for the whole infirmary. A very delicate environment. I'm Rod Nthn, the foreman. I'll have you know, I'm the first Thropinese to ever hold that position."

"Congratulations."

"I'm very important."

"That's great."

"I have a key to the Commodore Club."

"Oh really."

"The chairman of the board called me once."

"That's just super."

"And I can make announcements on the PA whenever I want."

"Tremendous."

"You have no idea."

"You're very special."

"Thank you," Rod said, curtsying and blushing all at once.

"Um, how do I get out of here?"

"I shall conduct you," said the Thropinese, bowing and offering one of his hideous bug legs for Pauline to take. She did. It felt like a skeleton's arm, except with spikes and mucus all over it. She tried not to gag. The creature led her through the machines, pausing to introduce her to several of the workers as his "new friend," until they reached a bank of elevators, one of which went to the first floor. It was this elevator that Rod Nthn stopped in front of, and he pushed the UP button.

They waited. And waited. For the next forty-five minutes, Rod Nthn paid Pauline many embarrassing compliments, exclaiming over her hazel eyes; her fiery red curls; the keenness of her fangs; her clear, chicken pox–free skin; and her dainty vampiric hands.

Finally, the elevator arrived. They were the only ones aboard; 6,199 buttons covered all the walls. Rod pressed the button to the first floor and stepped back. The elevator jolted once, then began to rise.

When they had just passed the 6,000th floor, Rod Nthn suddenly pressed the button for 5,999, where the elevator came to a slow, squeaky stop.

"What's going on?" said Pauline, growing more and more uncomfortable with this guy.

As the door opened, he dashed for Pauline, and before she could begin to react, the strange creature picked her up and hoisted her over his shoulder.

"Hey! Leggo!"

He whisked her out of the elevator, down a long, black hallway, through a pair of black swinging doors, and into his bachelor pad, where he seated her on a big throne made of bones and bottle caps, chained her ankles to the legs and her arms to the armrests, stood back, and said, in his annoying honking-cat voice:

"You are to be my wife."

"What?"

"To cook me stew and clean up my mess and listen to my troubles and accompany me to parties. Forever. Ha-ha-ha!"

Pauline fought against her restraints with such vigor that she nearly tipped the throne over.

"Stop that, now," said Rod, steadying the throne, then slapping Pauline once in the face.

"Ow," said Pauline, genuinely scared for the first time since she'd been here. Up till now, she'd just been incredulous. Now, she was frightened. "I'll bite you."

"Don't you know the Thropinese cannot be infected by vampiresses?"

"Look, Rod," said Pauline, glancing around the room, which was filled with white rubber furniture and modern-looking sculptures of black marble. "I think you're a nice fellow, but I need to get to the first floor. It's a matter of life and death."

He said, "Number one, chicken pox is not fatal, and number two, the chicken pox ward is not on the first floor.

That's where the chief of surgery's penthouse is; that's where Customs and Immigration is; that's where the big freight pipes are. There's nothing there for a vampiress. Especially not a *betrothed* vampiress."

Then Rod produced a small object seemingly out of nowhere: a green tube of some kind, tapered at one end, with writing on it too tiny to read.

"Look, my dearest one," he said, holding the object in the air. "My favorite Oppabof import. Superglue."

Pauline panicked. What the heck was he going to do? Glue her mouth shut? Her *eyes*? She was securely chained to the chair; there was no going *any*where. She would scream if he got near her face. She would *spit*.

But instead Rod Nthn got down on all sixes and began to crawl around the throne, squeezing globs of superglue where the chair legs met the floor.

"We can't have you tumbling over while I'm at work, now, can we?"

"Let me go."

"Now," said Rod Nthn, circling her throne and chuckling, "let me tell you about the festivities and menu I have planned for our nuptials."

CHAPTER 20

Chance had to find Yryssy Ayopy. *How?* He didn't even know how to get off the basement floor. He could find only two elevators—one firmly locked, the other broken and full of cardboard boxes. Next to the broken elevator was a door marked STAIRS, but it, too, was securely locked, and no amount of prying would compromise it.

If only he could ask someone.

Chance smacked himself on the forehead.

"Duh."

He plucked a torch out of its sconce and went up to the first cell he saw. Empty, the door wide open, the key in the lock. The next one contained a dead Balliope, and the third an actual vampire trying to jam his head through the bars. The fourth contained a particularly ugly Vyrndeet.

"Sir," said Chance. "Do you know where I can find Yryssy Ayopy?"

"Ew, a human," it said.

"She's a Geckasoft," said Chance. "She knows a lot of secrets."

"Never heard of her."

"Well, do you know to get off this floor?"

"The elevators are locked or broken. This place was not designed with the easy exit in mind."

Chance advanced to the next cage, in which an aged wizard sitting in a corner gave him the evil eye.

"Sir, do you—"

"I heard you. No, I don't know Yryssy Ayopy, and I don't know how to get out of the basement. So off with you."

Several hours later, Chance was about to give up when he heard a deep, rough voice.

"I know where she is," it said. The voice reminded Chance of cats' tongues and aquarium gravel. It was coming from the cell across the passageway.

"What?"

Chance turned to behold a creature that looked like a winged crash test dummy. It was crouching in a corner, its legs crossed, its arms akimbo.

"Oh, a human. What a disappointment."

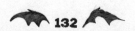

"I know, I know," said Chance. "Would you please tell me where Yryssy is?"

"Sure, no prob. She's on the . . . wait, oh darn, I . . . I'm having trouble remembering . . ."

Chance groaned. "But you said—"

"I might be able to remember if . . ."

"What? What!"

". . . I was freed from this cage."

"I, uh, don't know—"

"*You* got out somehow. At least I assume you're not here as a visitor. Do a fella a solid and get me out of here. And I will tell you where Porsyppy Papopy is. Furthermore, I will get you off this floor."

"Really?"

"Really."

"Have you got a chain in there?"

"No, no chain."

"Just a minute."

Chance jogged up and down the passageway until he found the open cell with the key in the lock. He jogged back.

"Let's hope this works," said Chance, plugging in the key and turning. A little WD-40 would've helped, but it worked.

"Thank you, human," the creature said, stretching and flapping its wings.

"Now can you please," said Chance, "take me to Yryssy."

"Well," said the creature, "I must admit I really don't

have any idea where she is. I've never even heard of her. I just wanted out *so bad.*"

Chance sat on the floor and put his head in his hands.

"Jeez, sorry," said the creature.

"Did you know," said Chance, "that everyone in this hospital will be dead in less than twenty-four hours unless I find Yryssy?"

"Oh dear, are you sure?"

"Positive," said Chance. He actually had no idea how soon it might be, but he did know time was of the essence. He was beginning to experience the chemical and physiological changes in his body that usually preceded a powerful cry.

"But listen," said the creature. "I *can* get you out of here. That part wasn't a lie."

"You can?"

"Follow me. What's your name, by the way?"

"Chance."

"I am Fer Dramwoot the Untidy, a proud and invulnerable Slipling."

The creature took a bow, then was off at a brisk pace, exercising its magnificent wings as they walked. Eventually, they came to the broken elevator, where the creature stopped.

"Ta-da!"

"This one is broken," said Chance.

The creature opened the doors. The elevator was still full of cardboard boxes.

"Come on, we're climbing through these boxes, upward."

After two hours of struggle, they reached the top layer of boxes. The shaft disappeared up into a blackness darker than starless space.

"Now what?" said Chance.

"Climb on," said the creature, crouching down so Chance could jump up on its back. "I hope you're not passing along any disease."

"I'm perfectly healthy."

"Good. Now, I don't think I can fly more than one hundred stories or so with a passenger, so I'll have to drop you off on one floor. Then, you're on your own. Ready?"

"Ready," said Chance. For the first time since he'd arrived here, the sweet aroma of confidence began to waft around him.

Fer Dramwoot the Untidy lifted off slowly and laboriously, rising higher, past the 6,240th floor, the 6,235th, the 6,230th, picking up speed, the 6,200th, the 6,190th, the 6,180th . . . Then the creature began to lose steam. At the 6,170th floor, he stopped, hovering in midair.

"This is as far as I can take you, Mr. Chance. Try to stay in the crawl spaces between floors, and use the air ducts to move up and down."

"Are you sure you don't know where I can find Yryssy Ayopy?" said Chance, climbing onto a five-inch ledge in front of the floor's closed double doors, from between which a shaft of light shone.

"No. But you will figure it out."

And with that, the Slipling continued upward until it disappeared into the murk in the distance.

Chance stood precariously on the ledge. He peered down. He couldn't see the bottom. Terror rose up into his esophagus, stopping there to throb. He could barely move. He peered through the one-eighth-inch crack between the doors. Figures strode by, unidentifiable sounds squeezed through. He tried to pry the doors apart but could not get a grip. Chance drew his trusty iron rod and tried to jam it between the doors, but it was too thick; besides, he couldn't get any leverage. He dared not cry for help; if he went back to the brig, they'd make sure he couldn't get out again.

The ledge went all the way around the inside of the elevator shaft. Chance turned his head as far as he could and noticed an object sitting on the ledge in the back right corner—a foot-long object of some kind standing straight up. What *was* that?

A hammer.

If only . . .

He had no choice. Chance began to shuffle along the edge so carefully, hugging the dirty wall, his cheek flat against it, while behind him an 800-foot plunge seemed to tug at his ankles. Inch by inch, he made his way toward the hammer. The closer he got, the more anxious he became.

Something stung the back of his neck. Chance slapped at it. He lost his balance. He pinwheeled his arms as fast as he could and just barely saved himself. He was breathing so hard he blew dust off the wall.

Out of the corner of his eye, he saw his attacker. Some kind of deformed June bug as big as a Ping-Pong ball. Even in the dark, Chance could make out its half-inch-long stinger. The beast orbited his head, looking for another place to strike. Chance shuffled along, filled with panic and fear. He was halfway to the hammer when the insect thing stung him in the ribs. All Chance could do was stifle a scream; he couldn't bat it away for fear of falling. It stayed stuck to his rib cage, leaving the stinger in his flesh for a full ten seconds before withdrawing it and flying away.

Chance got closer. The insect dive-bombed him and stung him near the hairline over his right eye. Then it hit in the same spot over his left eye. The swelling welts felt like white-hot marbles between his skin and skull.

He made it to the hammer. He carefully lifted up one leg, sideways, and bent his body in the other direction, as if he were doing a slow-motion cartwheel. He bent more and more until he could grasp the handle between two fingers, then righted himself. Slowly, cautiously, he began his return trip.

Halfway there, the creature stung him on the ankle. Chance roared through his teeth. Oh, how he wanted to crush that thing!

He shuffled along, a hairbreadth at a time. The insect seemed to have gotten bored, and it was no longer hovering

and darting and wheeling. When Chance finally reached the relative safety of the doors, he paused to catch his breath. He felt the lump on his side—nearly an inch high. He lifted up his shirt. The welt was a pulsing red monolith. He felt his forehead. The two bumps over his eyes, in his hairline, felt like they had risen even more than an inch. They throbbed like bad cuts, stinging like lime juice in the eye.

Chance stuck the claw end of the hammer between the doors and began to work it in deeper and deeper. He peered through the crack. No creatures in sight at the moment, and the sounds of activity seemed distant. He pried the doors open far enough to get his fingertips securely inside. He tucked the hammer through a belt loop.

Chance pulled apart the doors as hard as he could until they were open enough to squeeze his body through. He fell onto a hard, sandpapery, reddish-brown surface.

Chance would never know that at that exact instant, his sister Pauline was hurtling past him at 120 miles per hour, falling down the elevator shaft from which he had just freed himself.

He looked up.

Standing in a half circle around him were four Balliopes, all dressed in tennis outfits and holding rackets that looked too big for their little round frames. Tennis courts. Hundreds of them, stretching off into the brightly lit distance.

"Hey, you okay, bud?" said one of them, getting down on one knee.

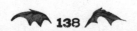

Why weren't they handcuffing him and hauling him off to jail?

"Yeah, you don't look so great," said another. "And you smell terrible, like you've been in a dungeon. Have you been in a dungeon, demon?"

"Oh, uh, no. Huh?"

"How in the world did you get *inside* a broken elevator shaft?" said the third. "Can't you read the sign?"

Chance turned around. On the elevator doors, a length of old, yellowed masking tape read in black Magic Marker: BROKEN PLEASE DON'T USE.

He also noticed his reflection in the polished doors. The bright red bumps on his forehead looked a little like . . . the horns of a demon.

"Uh, I think . . . um . . . well, I just wound up in there somehow. I don't know how it happened. I was just sitting in my room on the, uh, ingrown-toenail ward, uh, chatting with, uh, Yryssy Ayopy, and I think she maybe sneaked some knockout drops in my drink. Or something."

"Knockout drops work on demons?"

"Sometimes," said Chance.

The Balliopes nodded and stroked their scant yellow beards.

"Hmm," they all said.

"Yeah.

"What was the name? Assyria Karaoke?"

"Yryssy Ayopy."

"Never heard of her," said three of them. But the fourth said, "I have. She's in a coma, acute Iptid's Misery. My sister, who's a nurse, told me all about her. She's a goner. Yryssy, not my sister. No cure for Iptid's Misery."

"Oh no," said Chance. "Where is she now?"

"Room—"

Suddenly, a loud, electrified crackle sounded. A PA system.

> ***Attention: Human on premises. Cunning and wily. Location unknown. Jail escapee. Approach with extreme caution: danger of infection. Slight, brown hair, ears stick out. Disable or kill on sight.***

"Wow, that's the second time in a couple days," said a Balliope. "Place is just crawling with humans."

Chance could feel his ears turning red. If it weren't for these bug bites, Chance knew he would be on his way back to jail. If he ever found out where the flying beastie lived, he'd send it a fruit basket.

"It's probably the same human," said another Balliope. "The chances that two could get in are pretty slim."

"What's your name, demon?"

"Um, er . . . Jiro. What room did you say Yryssy Ayopy is in?"

"She's in 2222.001. I remembered the number easily because it's easy to remember."

"Do you know how to get back to the ingrown-toenail ward?" said a Balliope.

"No, but I can find my way," said Chance.

The red horns were beginning to throb less. He had to get away from these Balliopes. He was afraid that soon his brief disguise would disappear.

"We'll walk you to the right elevator. It's about a quarter mile, thataway.

"Oh, I think I can find it."

"C'mon, fellows. Let's get Jiro where he's going."

As they walked, Chance was certain his welts had reduced by at least a third. Maybe half.

Eventually, the Balliopes paused in front of a bank of elevators. One of them pressed the UP button to an elevator that went all the way to the 1,000th floor.

Fifteen minutes later, it finally came.

"Now, remember to get off at 3,190," said the Balliopes. "That's the ingrown-toenail ward."

Chance jumped into the vacant elevator, his back to the Balliopes. In order to press 3,190, he would have to turn around and face them. He put his arm up to his brow, said "*Bye, you guys, thanks,*" then pressed the CLOSE DOORS button. Before they shut completely, Chance thought two of the Balliopes' faces had darkened with quizzical looks.

The elevator rose. Chance punched 2,222. He studied his welts in the polished steel walls. They still looked like the horns of a demon, but not so dramatically. Chance

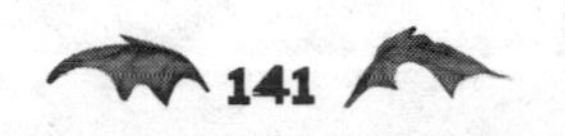

tapped them, squeezed them, worried them, flicked them, in hopes they would get re-inflamed so he could make it to 2,222 before someone recognized him as human, but his abuses seemed to do no good. Creatures started to board. As the elevator went higher and higher, longer and longer were the hard looks each being gave Chance. The elevator seemed to be stopping on every other floor, sucking creatures in, spitting them out. What was it, rush hour?

Then, finally 2,222.

"Excuse me," said Chance. "Coming out, coming out."

All the creatures looked at him. Just as he elbowed his way off the crowded elevator and the door began to close, someone said, "Hey, was that a demon? Or a h—?"

Then the door closed behind him.

Chance had to work fast.

The floor appeared to be a regular old hospital ward. There was nobody about, except for a short Vyrndeet dressed in a maid's uniform who was bent over a laundry hamper piled high with dirty sheets and towels. It walked into a room, never noticing Chance coming down the hall toward it. Chance took the opportunity to run as fast as he could toward the hamper, looking at room numbers as he went—odd numbers on the right, 2222.035, 2222.033, 2222.031—until he reached 2222.021, the room the maid was cleaning. Chance climbed into the hamper and buried himself deep in the towels and sheets. The smell reminded Chance of wet tennis balls. He waited. He felt his forehead; the welts were nearly gone.

Presently the maid came out of the room, tossed laundry on top of the pile, and pushed the cart to the next room on the same side of the hall: 2222.019. Again, Chance waited. He didn't dare peek out of the hamper, as he could hear the murmurs and honks and snarls and whimpers of beings walking back and forth.

Chance checked his pocket to make sure the plastic pouch of flerk was still there, that it hadn't leaked. Ten minutes later, the hamper moved again: 2222.017. Only eight more to go till he reached Yryssy—

Ktzzzkrkpop! went the PA system.

Attention: Update.

Here we go again, he thought.

Human spotted, Floor 2,222, human spotted, Floor 2,222. Local agents, please respond with deadly force.

This was getting old. The floor suddenly thundered with the commotion of what Chance assumed to be "local agents."

The maid had moved the laundry cart to 2222.015. Chance listened to the security guards shouting and slamming doors. Then the cart was by 2222.013. The laundry bore down on Chance, heavier and heavier. Chance held his breath. His entire left leg fell asleep. The hamper moved one room closer roughly every ten minutes.

The security-guard search party seemed to be wrapping up—orders were no longer barked, boots no longer stomped, whistles no longer pealed, golf carts no longer screeched. He risked peeking out of the hamper. *There: Room 2222.001!* And no one visible in the hall except for a few distant figures. Chance silently unburied himself and tried to climb out of the hamper, but his leg was still asleep, so he fell hard on the linoleum. He recovered, flattened his body against the hallway floor, and peeked into the hospital room. Chance didn't see the maid. *Ah.* There it was in the bathroom, its back to him. Chance glanced at the gurney. A strange creature, like E.T. except light gray and a bit more muscular, lay in a coma under a thin sheet, tubes and lines coming from its body. It looked exactly as Simon had described.

Yryssy Ayopy.

Chance sneaked into the room and quickly, silently slid under Yryssy's gurney. He climbed up into the framework under the mattress, where he could hide. The maid cleaned the bathroom and changed the sheets and emptied the wastebaskets. It finished its task and left, closing the door. All was quiet except for the chuff of a machine pumping something into the tubes leading to Yryssy's body. Chance did not want to know what that something was.

He carefully extricated himself from the gurney's framework and stood next to the comatose creature.

"Yryssy?" whispered Chance, taking the little capsule of flerk out of his pocket. "Can you hear me?"

Yryssy did not respond. Chance shook her by her skinny, almost nonexistent shoulders, but she didn't stir. *Maybe it's best she's comatose; she might panic in the presence of a human and refuse the flerk*, he thought.

"Okay, I'm going to give you some medicine," whispered Chance. "Then, you'll wake up and make some Ypocrasyne and give it to Dave Green. Got it?"

Chance pried her lipless gray mouth open, revealing tiny purple teeth, rows and rows of them, all the way to the back of her throat. Her breath reeked of burned meat. Chance held the little bubble of flerk between his thumb and forefinger, forced it as far into her slobbery mouth as he could, then squeezed the little plastic capsule until it popped, releasing all the flerk into her mouth. Then Chance rubbed her throat, like one would do with a dog given a pill, until she swallowed, once, then twice.

Chance's job was done. Now all he had to do was find Arbipift Obriirpt, get the map, then get the heck out of this place.

He heard voices outside the door. Chance dropped to the ground, rolled under the gurney, and climbed back up into the framework. Above him, Yryssy did not stir. Maybe it took a while for flerk to take effect.

Chance watched as two sets of feet very much like the legs of small three-legged stools, came into the room, their owners conversing, one pushing a cart.

". . . a dumb Vyrndeet accused me of cheating at the egg-and-spoon race, and now it's asking me out!"

"The nerve. What'd you tell it?"

"To go jump in a lake of fire. Okay, how many vials of ichor are we taking today?"

"I can't remember. Check the chart. Room 2222.001, Ayopy, Yryssy. Weird; yesterday, this room was guarded and chock-full of Balliopes and official creatures."

"Wait. Lemme see the chart. Oh look. This is yesterday's."

"No way."

"Way. *Here's* today's chart. Looks like Ayopy was transferred out of this room, to an undisclosed location. This is Mrs. Bdeebee Rurriery. She just happens to be a Geckasoft, too."

The blood in Chance's veins seemed to slow to a complete stop then begin to freeze. He could barely breathe.

He had failed. He had failed Simon, Yryssy, the entire population of the infirmary, himself, and his dad, who was surely watching from the domain of the afterlife.

CHAPTER 21

While Rod Nthn puttered around his bachelor pad, straightening up, polishing statues, and arguing on the telephone with florists and caterers over prices and scheduling, Pauline watched from her bone-and-bottle-cap throne, trying to come up with a way out. Nothing. Her ankles and wrists were tightly bound to the throne, and the throne itself was glued to the floor. Pauline tried to summon Mersey, but to no avail.

Suddenly, the whine of audio feedback could be heard, faintly, coming from the black hall beyond Rod's swinging doors. She struggled to listen, but distance and Rod's voice—he was still on the phone—kept obscuring the PA system announcement.

At . . . ion

". . . or my name isn't Rod Nthn, I won't pay 340 clahd for Oppaboffian dandelions . . ."

Hu . . . n spo . . . ed . . . Fl . . . r . . .

". . . hate the smell of gorbyroot buds . . ."

hu . . . otted, Fl . . . 2,222

". . . outrageously overpriced . . ."

Lo . . . al a . . . nts, pl . . . r . . . nd

". . . not flowers, you weedmongers . . ."

wi . . . deadly . . . orce.

". . . good day and good-bye!"

Rod slammed the phone down, the old-fashioned kind with a round dial and a cradle.

"The nerve!" shouted Rod.

Pauline was trying to piece together the fragments of

the PA announcement. She was pretty sure about the *deadly force* part. But another part—*hu . . . otted fl . . . 2,222*—what the heck did that mean? Huge slotted flowchart? Humid besotted floozy?

Wait.

Human spotted, floor 2,222.

Pauline had to get out of there. If they caught Chance, it would all be over. But Chance was a clever hider. One time he'd hidden *in* a couch. He had unstapled the thin cloth lining underneath and crawled up into the belly. No one would've found him if Dad hadn't sat on the couch, squeezing a yelp out of Chance.

Pauline was struck by an itch at the tip of her nose. At least her head wasn't restrained; she could bend over to scratch with her fingernail. As she straightened up, she got an idea.

Rod was busy sorting silverware in the kitchen, not paying Pauline the least mind. She bent down again and, with some effort, pulled off Mersey's fangs, gripping them in the palm of her hand.

"Hey, Rod," she called. "C'mere."

"What is it, my sweet?"

"I have to show you something."

Rod heaved a great sigh of impatience, but came over to Pauline. She stared at him. He stared back.

"What?" said Rod.

Pauline smiled, revealing fangless teeth.

"You're . . . ," said Rod, eyes widening, jaw slackening, cheeks reddening, ". . . a *human*?"

"Yes, I am, and don't you know we humans can spit thirty feet, and I've got an infection that will kill a Thropinese in minutes."

"You can? You do?"

"So you better make your way over here, slowly, and unshackle me. Or I'll infect ya, and you'll die writhing in agony. *Writhing*."

"But . . . but . . . dear, I don't care if you're human, or diseased. I love you anyway. We're to be husband and wife. I didn't realize you were so unhappy. What can I do?"

Pauline answered by leaning forward and baring her teeth in a spitting posture.

"Okay, okay, I've got my key. I'm coming."

After Rod freed Pauline, she shackled him to his own throne. She left the key by the dishwasher and put her fangs back in.

"And no screaming, or I'll come back and spit in your eye. Remember, we humans have ultrasensitive hearing, too—I'll be able to hear you forty floors away."

"Oh dear."

"Now, tell me how to get to the 2,222nd floor."

Rod told her.

"Don't let anyone know I'm in this hospital, or I'll come back and—"

"I know! I know!"

And Pauline took her leave of Rod Nthn.

Pauline found elevator bank 85, pushed the UP button, and waited for the car that went all the way to 2,134. The elevator finally arrived, discharging its cargo of creatures, none of which paid her any attention. Pauline jumped on.

The upward journey was repeatedly interrupted by creatures embarking and disembarking. Pauline kept her teeth bared, so there was no mistaking her as a human. She prayed no real vampires would get on.

At one point, the doors opened and in strode a pair of Vyrndeets, one short, one tall, in the middle of a conversation, the shorter pushing a stroller.

And in the stroller was a toddler vampire. When it saw Pauline, it opened its mouth and pointed at her.

"Hooma," it said, its needlelike fangs showing. They were a bit crooked. *Someone* was going to need braces. "Hooma."

Pauline turned away and froze, watching the floors as they slowly went by. *If this kid outs me . . .*

The taller Vyrndeet said to the shorter, "I'm going to Bholph's to get my fur done, maybe some blond highlights here and there. Come with me, Dirgette."

"Wooky," said the little bloodsucker. "Hooma."

"Oh, Bholph's is way too expensive for me, Pipth," said Dirgette.

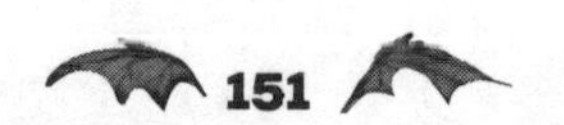

"You ought to quit babysitting and come work for me," said Pipth. "I could use a paralegal, and you'd make three times what you're getting now."

The vampire baby reached around and grabbed Dirgette's leather leggings and began to tug.

"Dirgie, wook, hooma."

"Yeah, but I love kids," she said, reaching down to remove the tiny hands yanking on her leggings. "Even little Marvoob here, who tries my patience. Isn't that right, Marvoobie?"

"Hooma," said Marvoob, pointing at Pauline. "Bah."

"What's he saying?" said Pipth.

"No clue. Marvoob, please be quiet."

But Marvoob began to wail. He reached for Pauline, his slender fingers only inches away from her jeans.

"Hoomahoomahooma. No."

"I think he said, *Whom a who ma hoomano.*"

"That doesn't make any sense."

"Toddlers don't make much sense. That's their job."

"Bah hooma."

A Thropinese on the elevator piped up.

"I think the baby's saying *human*," it said.

"He wouldn't know that word," said Dirgette.

"There *is* a human loose. Maybe the kid saw it."

"They didn't catch it?"

"Waah, hooooooma."

"No, it must've escaped the 2,222nd floor somehow," said the Thropinese. "Could be anywhere now."

"I bet it's still there, but those dumb Balliopes couldn't find him."

"Hey," said a Balliope, who was hidden in a corner. "Take that back."

"Sorry."

"Speaking of 2,222," said Dirgette, "here we are. Who's getting off?"

"Me," said Pauline.

"Hooma!"

The doors opened. Pauline found herself on the very floor she hoped and prayed her little brother was hidden on.

CHAPTER 22

The two nurses left the room. With the Geckasoft above him metabolizing the only centiliter of flerk left on the planet, Chance Bee Jeopard, hiding in the framework of the gurney, began to cry for real.

Dave Green was out there somewhere, dying, in his fist the ruin of Saint Philomene's Infirmary for Magical Creatures. Chance would have to find him and wrench the vial from his hand.

Impossible.

Chance was truly tuckered out. He began to drift off.

"You'll be out of surgery and eating Jell-O in less than two hours, Mrs. Rurriery."

Chance woke.

"You like Jell-O, don't you, Mrs. Rurriery?"

He was in motion. The gurney in whose framework he was nestled rode smoothly down a light blue hallway, guided by a creature with skinny, chickenlike legs shod in glittery orthopedic footwear.

The creature was speaking gently to the gurney's occupant above him, Mrs. Rurriery, the Geckasoft in whose mouth Chance had squeezed the flerk, and who was now apparently on her way to have an operation.

How long had he been asleep?

"Mrs. Rurriery, did you know the chief of surgery himself is going to remove your kidney boulders? You're going to feel so much better."

They took a sharp left and then stopped. Chance dared to peek out.

They were in an operating room filled with stainless steel and bright light and creatures in green scrubs. They moved Mrs. Rurriery from the gurney onto an operating table. Then someone moved the gurney into the hallway, which was teeming with creatures.

A golf cart raced past Chance and down the hallway, the driver shouting *"Delivery for Mr. Bee, delivery for Mr. Bee!"*

The voice sounded familiar. Chance looked out as the

golf cart sped away down the hall. Just as it was rounding a corner, he saw the driver's curly mass of fiery red hair. Then the cart was gone.

Could it be? If that *was* Pauline, how in the world did she get here? Why was she here? To get him? Chance hoped not. If he had somehow inadvertently involved his sister . . . He shuddered.

He had to act now. He might never see her again. And they needed each other, now more than ever. Chance decided to make a run for it.

Pauline was nowhere in sight. He sped down the hallway, racing past gasping, pointing, shouting, screaming creatures, following what he hoped was his sister's path through the maze of corridors, listening for the *squeenk* of tires on polished linoleum, watching for flashes of red hair—

There! One hundred yards ahead, just turning a corner—Pauline. Chance picked up speed. Beings were starting to chase him now, and still others tried to trip or tackle him as he ran by, but most just ducked into their sanctuaries—rooms, supply closets, laboratories, bathrooms—and slammed their doors behind them.

Chance rounded a corner. There she was, fifty yards ahead.

"Delivery for Mr. Bee!"

"Mr. Bee, here!" shouted Chance. She didn't seem to hear. He was nearly out of breath. "Pauline!"

She looked over her shoulder. Chance frantically gesticulated.

"I'm coming, hold on!" she shouted.

Pauline accomplished an excellent three-point turn and accelerated toward him.

Then, Balliopes. Half a dozen of them with halberds and weighted nets poured out of a doorway, Chet leading the way.

"I remember you, human," said Chet.

There was no way to get past them. Chance stopped, and he put up his hands.

"Don't spear me, I give up," shouted Chance. But still the Balliopes came for him, halberds lowered and ready to pierce. Chance was about to turn and flee when he noticed some of them were airborne.

Pauline had driven right through them at top speed, scattering them like tenpins.

"Get on," she said when she pulled up next to Chance. He jumped into the passenger's seat. He had never been so glad to see his sister. He had never been so glad to see a *human*.

"Now what!" said Pauline and Chance at the same time.

"I don't know!" they said, also at the same time.

Pauline took a quick turn down a short, vacant hallway, at the end of which were the open doors of what looked like a large event room.

"Dead end," said Chance.

Pauline drove right in.

It was a theater.

It was empty except for a few folding chairs. A beautiful red velvet curtain framed the stage.

"Come on," said Pauline, jamming on the brakes just in time to avoid crashing into the stage. "See that air vent in the ceiling?"

"We can't reach that."

"Grab a few chairs," she said, ignoring him. "Put them on top of one another, just under the vent. Hurry."

Chance grabbed three and helped his sister stack them up. *There's no way this will work,* thought Chance. *Our foes will easily see where we went.*

Pauline carefully climbed the chairs. Security was getting closer, and the PA was now blasting updates. She reached the ceiling and popped out the vent.

Then she dropped it to the floor.

"What are you *doing*?" hissed Chance, looking behind him. He was waiting for security to come barreling around the corner, signaling the end of their adventure and the beginning of their life sentences in the basement.

Then his sister climbed down.

"Pauline!"

"Now, let's hide behind one of the big doors by the entrance," Pauline whispered, just as Chance opened his mouth to protest. "Come on."

They ran toward the doors, hiding behind them as the security force arrived. More Balliopes, Chet leading the way, as well as a fifteen-foot ogre that had to stoop to get into the room.

"Curses," said Chet. "Up in the air ducts. They'll be hard to find. You, Bweetoy, and you, Jim. In the ducts, now! Find them!"

Two Balliopes climbed the stack of chairs and disappeared into the air duct. The rest of the security team marched out, never noticing Chance and Pauline.

The two young Jeopards held their breaths for a full minute before Pauline signaled the all clear, then rushed up and gave her brother a hug. Chance noticed his sister was prominently fanged.

"How . . . how . . . ," Chance started to say.

"We'll talk about it later. Now, we need to hide for real. Look, what's behind that door?"

There was a black door near one corner of the theater. It opened onto a room that smelled of wax and hand soap. They shut the door and breathed a collective sigh of relief.

The small room was painted black and lined on the left side by racks of clothes and costumes, and on the right with two vanities whose mirrors were surrounded by lightbulbs. Pauline flipped a switch below one of the mirrors, bringing the powerful bulbs to bright life and illuminating the two white vanities covered with small glass jars of colorful powders and creams, hairbrushes, hair clips, lipsticks, and other materials used to bring forth in living color the stage actor.

Pauline sat at one vanity and Chance at the other. Over the next hour, they discussed how the last couple of days had unfolded, how each of them came to be where they were now.

"You really worried me, sibling," said Pauline. "You know, Mom is out of town. We have to be home before she gets back."

"Oh, I forgot!"

"She was kind of upset she didn't get to say good-bye."

"I had to come here."

"Oh, here's one more thing," said Pauline. "I'm in contact with Mersey—sometimes—and she can intercept signals from communications devices here through a website whose owner is located in Rincón Oscuro, which is right over the infirmary. Walkie-talkies and such. Like the security forces here use."

"No kidding. How do you communicate?"

Pauline explained the curious properties of broken fulgurite segments.

"You don't even have to talk into it. It's here in my pocket. Except I haven't heard from Mersey for quite a while now."

"You hear her voice in your head?"

"Yeah."

"Maybe the fulgurite isn't close enough," said Chance. "Try holding it next to your ear."

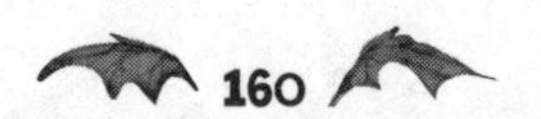

Pauline didn't think it would work, but she did as her brother suggested.

"Mersey?" said Pauline.

Is that . . . you? Pauline? I—

"Mersey, I found Chance. He came down to Saint Philomene's Infirmary for Magical Creatures to save the place. There's a madman somewhere in here threatening to unleash a lethal virus that will kill the entire population of one point eight million."

Omigosh. Where is he? The madman?

"We don't know. We thought maybe you could help."

I did record a mysterious conversation about an hour ago. I couldn't make any sense of it. I'll play it for you. Just a sec.

Pauline found a sewing kit in the vanity drawer, and with a doubled length of strong thread, she made a necklace out of the fulgurite.

Here's the recording, said Mersey. *It's not perfect.*

It featured two new voices, one a plangent screech unlike anything she'd ever heard; the other was human. Strange sounds, whizzes and chirrs and whooshes, interrupted the conversation, which Pauline repeated word for word for her brother's benefit.

"I've told you, we're doing everything we—"

"—and I've been awake for three full days—"

"—be patient, we—"

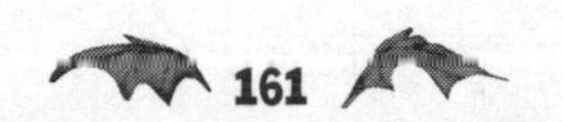

"—the fever's start—now—means I've got no m—than a few hours to live. You have to help me. My mind . . ."

"Will you at least tell me where you are?"

"I can't—"

"—but how w—we find you if—"

"I'm not far. You radio me when she's rea—and I'll tell you wh—to go."

"But—"

"And remem—, if I am harass—in—, I will turn this bug loose, Bittius."

"Why would we har—"

"I am being harassed by demons every time I blink. Now good—"

"Please don't—, Mr. Gr—"

Then, silence.

"Mersey, is that the end of the recording?"

That's it.

"What were all those strange sounds in the background?"

No idea.

"Chance, who's Bittius?" said Pauline.

"That's the chairman of the infirmary board," he said, leaning on the vanity, his head in his hands. "And Mr. Gr—is, I'm pretty sure, Mr. Green. Dave Green."

"The one holding the virus."

Chance nodded, squeezing his head between his palms. "Dave Green is dying of something called GIGI. It causes you to lose your mind before it kills you. It sounds like he doesn't have much time left to live. And when he does go, he'll somehow release the virus.

"Well, obviously someone's got to stop him," said Pauline. "And who is this *she* Dave Green referred to?"

"That's Yryssy Ayopy," said Chance, standing up and beginning to pace the small room. "The only one that can cure him. Except—"

"Except she's in a coma," finished Pauline. "And she can't be cured without flerk, which, unfortunately, wound up in another being."

Chance had never been so ashamed.

"But it wasn't your fault, Chance," said Pauline, stopping her brother in his tracks, taking him by the shoulders, and staring hard into his eyes. "Anyone would've made the same mistake. Look, all we have to do now is catch Dave Green and take away his vial of death."

"Ha!" said Chance bitterly.

"Mersey, any ideas?" said Pauline.

I'm tuned in, said Mersey. *If anyone uses those radios, I'll hear. And I'll report back to you.*

CHAPTER 23

Pauline no longer heard her friend talking in her head. As much comfort as having a connection to the outside world gave Pauline, she still did not much like having a voice in the middle of her brain that spoke of its own free will. Just as Pauline breathed a sigh of relief, the door to the room opened.

In strode a creature that looked like a five-foot meerkat: furless, clothed in slacks and a tunic made from supple purple plastic. When it saw Chance and Pauline, it shrieked. And when Chance and Pauline saw the strange creature, they shrieked.

"Don't hurt me," the creature said, holding out its gnarled hands, which reminded Chance of the antlers of a small deer. "I'm just an old actor with a love of the stage, and I bear no ill will toward vampiresses or humans. Seriously. Er, you're not contagious, are you? With something . . . unpleasant?"

"No. And we're not going to hurt you," said Chance, realizing he and his sister somehow had the upper hand. "Why don't you sit on the couch for a minute."

The creature tiptoed toward a ratty old divan missing a cushion and sat down. He smiled at the two Jeopards, who shuffled their feet and studied the floor, the lightbulbs, the makeup, the wardrobe, anything but the creature.

"Who . . . ?" said Chance.

"Why, I'm Braig Toop, retired physician," said the creature. "You probably have not seen many of my kind. I'm a Wreau. We Wreaux are members of the endangered species list."

While the Wreau sat on the divan, moving only to chew a long, curling fingernail, Chance and Pauline conferred in whispers.

"What do we do with him?"

"I don't know. I've never had anyone afraid of me before."

"I have an idea."

Pauline turned to their companion.

"Mr. Toop, are you aware of the urgent situation this infirmary is in right now?"

"Please call me Braig. Do you mean the budget deficit? Or the diaper shortage?"

"I guess that's a *no*," said Chance.

"Not another plumber's strike?"

"No, no," said Pauline. "Do you know who Dave Green is?"

"Never heard of him. Sounds human. A friend of yours?"

"No, not a friend. But he is a human."

"Humans have always gotten a bad rap down here. Well, not always; it was many years ago when a human showed up here accidentally—she had, by pure chance, fallen into a breached freight pipe. It turned out she was carrying some kind of germ that infected about a third of the population, several hundred of whom died. Since then, humans have been criminalized, even though we've long since found a cure for the disease. It's too bad."

Braig explained that he had grown up in the infirmary. His mother was a dentist, his father a podiatrist, and both had lived in the hospital their whole adult lives.

"They got married in a mineral spa on the water-therapy floor," Braig said. He grinned pleasantly. So did Chance and Pauline.

Nobody moved for a moment. Brother and sister glanced at each other.

"What have we got to lose by trusting this guy?" whispered Chance to his sister.

"Everything," she whispered back. "But he's also our best chance."

"Braig," said Pauline, "everyone in Saint Philomene's Infirmary for Magical Creatures is in serious danger."

And the two Jeopards told him everything.

"So," said Chance, "what do we do? Any ideas?"

The strange Wreau leaned back on the divan and closed his eyes. He stayed that way for a long time.

CHAPTER 24

Braig leaped up in one swift motion.

"I do have an idea," he said. "I need to make a call first."

The telephone sat on a small table half hidden under a rack of costumes. He dialed a number. "Hello?" someone answered.

"Muge, Braig here."

"Oh, hey, Braig, whassup."

"You know, livin' the dream."

"What can I do for you?"

"A little favor. Check the computer directory and find out where a patient named Yryssy Ayopy is."

"Yryssy . . . Ayopy . . . let's see . . . ah. Here she is. Location: Classified."

"Oh great."

"What's the big deal?" said Muge.

"I need to know where she is. It's critical. Life and death."

"Serious?"

"Like a heart attack."

"All right. Let me call you back in a bit."

Twenty interminable minutes later, Muge called back.

"Found her. Room 2250.984."

"Great! How'd you figure it out?"

"Easy. A quick search of the directory reveals only six beings here whose locations are classified. I made a list of these and ran it against the lists of occupied, unoccupied, and abandoned rooms, which account for all the rooms, except for, of course, six. I just called the room phones in all these "classified" locations. Five answered, all male. Logic dictates the sixth room, 2250.984, belongs to Yryssy Ayopy, Geckasoft, female."

"Muge, I owe you a roast Loyoy dinner."

"What's this all about, anyway?"

"I hope you never have to find out," said Braig. "But do yourself a favor. Get out of Saint Philomene's. Now."

"What for?"

"Trust me. Get out. I mean in the next ten minutes."

Braig hung up.

"Chance," he said, "any idea who performed the surgery on Mrs. Rurriery?"

"I remember a nurse saying the chief of surgery would be operating on her."

"Chief of surgery?" said Braig. "Feargus M'Quiminy? I find it hard to believe *he'd* be participating in something as routine as kidney boulders. But let's find out."

Braig called directory assistance. They put him through to Feargus M'Quiminy.

"Big Chief here," said M'Quiminy.

"Feargie, Braig Toop."

"Who?"

"Br—"

"Wait, don't tell me. Doctor, Wreau, specialist in blood, lymph, and ichor, rather ordinary sort, avocational actor, retired, old?"

"Er . . . yes," said Braig, shifting uncomfortably on the ratty old divan. "That's me."

"What can I do for you, Toop?"

"I understand you performed a boulderectomy on a certain Mrs. Rurriery today."

"And why is this of concern to an antique retired non-surgeon of modest professional acumen?"

"Well, with your permission, I'd like to, er, interview her."

"Denied. Good day."

M'Quiminy hung up.

"Well," said Braig, "he's forcing our hand. Chance, I'll need your help. But first, we must disguise you."

"How?" said Chance.

"We're going to turn you into a Euvyd, a very human-looking nonhuman. They have a pair of bright blue ears that stick out somewhat; translucent hair, like fiber-optic filaments; and a forehead run through with black, spidery veins. Now the ears are no problem—there's plenty of blue makeup here—but what to do about the rest?"

"Hey," said Pauline, "why not just wrap his head in cloth and dab something red on there to look like blood? So he looks like a Euvyd that's been in an accident? That would cover his hair and his forehead."

"A grand idea."

And so Pauline painted one of Chance's ears with sky-blue eye shadow, and Braig painted the other. They dressed his head in a large magician's handkerchief and made it gory with a tube of stage blood.

"Excellent," said Braig. "Now, all you need is a Kippetore hair shirt and a pair of galligaskins. And I happen to know we have both here in this room, as I played the role of Mogte in *The Late Great Golden Euvyd* last year (we could find no real Euvyd with sufficient acting ability to play the part) and I had to wear exactly that outfit. Look, here it is."

Chance donned the baggy leather and the uncomfortable Kippetore hair shirt.

"Good," said Braig. "Now we need some rope. About ten feet."

They looked. No rope.

"Hey," said Chance, opening a small leather suitcase full of leather belts. "How about a couple of these? We could just string them together."

"Yet another grand idea," said Braig, putting on a surgeon's costume. "Now, let's go, Chance."

"Wait," said Pauline. "What about me?"

"I need you to stay here, my dear," said Braig. "Would you get on the phone and try to find out where Dave Green is?"

"How in the world will I do that?" said Pauline, who did not want to be separated from her brother again so soon, or to be alone in a dark and spooky dressing room.

"I know you'll think of something."

"But . . . but what are you guys going to do?" said Pauline.

"We're going to fetch Mrs. Rurriery."

Then Braig, the Wreau, and Chance, the "Euvyd," were gone.

CHAPTER 25

Mersey," Pauline said to the empty room. "I need you."

Mersey did not answer. Could she be asleep? Had she lost her fulgurite? They had talked less than an hour before.

Pauline stared at the telephone, its round dial like an open mouth full of little circular teeth. She picked up the receiver, listened to the old-fashioned dial tone, then dialed zero.

"Directory assistance."

"Uh, have you got a listing for a Dave Green, um, ghoul?"

"Please hold."

Pauline listened to the distant clicks and chimes and hums of the subterranean telephonic grid until the operator came back on.

"Unknown," said the operator, and hung up. Pauline immediately called back, hoping for a different operator.

"Directory assistance."

"Uh, hello?"

"You again?"

"Uh, yes, can you connect me to an Oppabof operator?"

The operator laughed and hung up.

Pauline was not often stumped. In fact, this might have been the first time in her whole life a problem had been presented to her to which she could see no solution. *How does one find someone hiding in a six-thousand-floor building?*

Pauline thought hard. If Dave Green knew Yryssy Ayopy was in Room 2250.984, then he would not stray far from that floor. And if he *didn't* know where she was, it would make sense for him to wait right in the middle of the building, where the shortest average distance to any place in the infirmary would be. Sir Amk Bittius IV would have thought of all this, too, and would have security personnel vigorously searching these areas.

Or maybe not. Dave Green did say that if he was harassed, he would turn the virus loose.

But if he did that, he'd certainly never be cured. So assuming Bittius was acting on the same reasoning, he probably *did* have security hunting Dave Green. They might

not be able to do anything with him if they found him, but they would be better off knowing where he was.

Dave Green probably *did* know where Yryssy Ayopy was. After all, with the power he held in one hand, he could have pretty much whatever he wanted, crazy or not, and all he would've had to do was ask Bittius where Yryssy was. And Bittius would have told him.

Pauline figured Dave Green would be close to 2250.984. Pauline estimated this to be three hundred feet in any direction. That was a lot of ground to cover.

Pauline?

"Mersey, thank heavens!"

Pauline, I'm so glad you're there! Listen, just a few minutes ago, I recorded another conversation between Dave Green and Bittius. You can hear the same whizzes and whirrs as before. Listen:

"Mr. Green, Yryssy Ayopy is, um, coming out of her coma, so please make your way to Room 2250.984."

"You're lying, Bittius."

"Oh no, I'm not."

"Then give her the radio."

"Um, well, she's not completely conscious yet—"

"What a whopper."

"Mr. Green, you're not yourself, I—"

"From here on out, the only person I'll take a call from is Yryssy Ayopy."

"What could those background sounds be?" said Pauline. "Whatever they are, they're the key to finding him."

He sounds very ill, said Mersey. *I think we're running out of time. Is Chance with you?*

Pauline explained that Chance had left with their new and untested acquaintance, Braig, to find a certain Geckasoft, Mrs. Rurriery.

"I can't stay here anymore," Pauline said, jumping up from the vanity and looking around for anything she could take along on her journey through the 2200s. "I have to at least look for Dave Green."

But where?

"He must be traveling by stairs or air ducts. So I'm going to start looking on the 2,280th floor. Or, that's to say, the space *between* the 2,279th and 2,280th floors."

But he could be on 2,250 just as easily.

"I think they would've searched that floor already," said Pauline, going through the pockets of some of the costumes. In the pocket of the softest fur coat she'd ever felt, she found a handful of change. Clahd. Tarnished silver ten-clahd pieces, dull bronze five-clahd coins with holes in the center, a scatter of bluish-black clahd pennies, and a single one hundred–clahd piece as large and thin as a Pringle and made of pure gold. Pauline dumped it all in her front pocket,

except for a single ten-clahd piece, entirely untarnished and mirror-shiny, which she kissed once and dropped in her back pocket for luck.

"Mersey, when this is all over, I hope you'll tell me about Josh."

Mersey was quiet for a second.

I'll tell you everything.

Having someone speak directly in your brain amplifies every tonal nuance, and Pauline noted her friend's dejected tone.

Signing off for now, said Mersey.

Pauline left a note in lipstick on a vanity mirror in case Braig and Chance came back:

Looking for DG between 2,280 and 2,279, working my way up.

She had always wanted to write something on a mirror in red lipstick.

She dropped the lipstick in her pocket.

Outside in the theater, the golf cart was gone. The doors she had come through were open. She walked down the hallway baring her fangs, keeping a close eye out for real vampires.

Every so often, she'd mark a red-lipstick X on a wall.

She took the first elevator she found down to the 2,279th floor. It opened onto a narrow, dark hallway. It took her eyes a moment to adjust. Directly across from her was a door with a small green glass window. Before she opened it, she made a lipstick X at eye level on the wall beside the door. She stepped through the door, made another X on the other side, and found herself on a narrow balcony looking down into a huge open space.

Huge.

It was hundreds of stories deep and thousands of feet in width, and in the midst of the space flew hot-air balloons; little flying-saucer-like craft; toy helicopters; and huge bird-like beasts not unlike pterodactyls, each making sounds similar to those Pauline had heard on the recording Mersey had played her.

This was where Dave Green was hiding. Right out in the open, somewhere.

CHAPTER 26

The immense, empty space dominated the center of Saint Philomene's Infirmary for Magical Creatures. Middlespace was an open area in the shape of a stick of butter that was more than a third of a mile in breadth and more than a mile and a quarter deep. Around each of the seven hundred surrounding floors Middlespace took up was a balcony from which creatures could gaze. The space was placid and harmonious, and many beings spent time meditating on the balconies or watching the activities through one of the many telescopes, which cost merely one thin clahd to operate for a full thirty minutes. Once a week on the bottom floor, an orchestra assembled and played beautiful music that reached every floor in the acoustically perfect space.

Creatures flew kites, paper planes, and radio-operated helicopters; they blew bubbles and watched helium balloons float to the ceiling; huge Blutch spiders spun webs in the corners; great winged Flok'embles sailed through the air, chasing insects and smaller birds; lesser Perdelids glided on updrafts.

Flightless creatures could ride out into Middlespace on teacup-shaped open-air craft called jelsairs, which were provided by the infirmary's Parks and Recreation Department for a nominal rental fee. For a bit more, hot-air balloons could also be rented for a full day or more, some with large baskets designed to carry a dozen creatures, some that held two or three, and some that held just one being; the last was merely a seat-belted armchair equipped with a small flame jet to heat the air in the balloon and a quiet fan that could be used to serenely navigate around the space.

Middlespace was so large that it produced its own weather: Clouds would sometimes form around the 2,000th floor, occasionally gray-green ones that exploded into crackling thunder and torrents of rain and hung with fleeting chandeliers of blue and pink lightning. When the storms ended, the jelsairs and Flok'embles and balloons of all sizes that had been forced to take shelter would repopulate the fresh, clean rain-washed air in Middlespace.

It was in one of the small one-creature balloon-chairs that Dave Green, international chess master (FIDE rating 2296), GIGI sufferer, military biochemist, possessor of a small vial, was presently seated. His right hand gripped the vial, holding it over the edge of the chair so that if he were to die, his hand would go limp and let the vial go, and it would plummet a mile and explode on the hard floor below. No one knew where Dave was, no one could hurt him, and no one could stop him. When it was time, Yryssy would radio Dave, who would reveal his location, which Yryssy Ayopy would fly to in a jelsair to cure him. At that time, he would simply float to a balloon station, disembark—vial still firmly in hand—and have Bittius personally escort him to a pipe that would carry him back to the Lubbock, Texas, Dumpster whence he'd come.

Dave floated in Middlespace, still disguised as a ghoul, careful not to lose his grip on the vial and careful not to drop the radio into space. Both of those scenarios spelled doom for Dave.

Dave's greatest enemy was sleep. He had been floating out here without shut-eye for a long, long time, and sleep now heartily tugged at his eyelids. The fever—an indicator that the end was but a few hours away—had started a short

while before. Now it throbbed like a tiny magnetar in the center of his brain.

The balloon imperceptibly rose and fell and rotated while toy helicopters whizzed by and jelsairs darted this way and that. Flok'embles swooped and dove, hunting, sometimes curling into balls and dropping a thousand feet before unfurling and landing gently on the floor of Middlespace, where they would pluck at their breast feathers and utter their distinctive *icawk-awk* at the patrons crowding the cafés and at the children swimming in pools of blue-green water and at the Balliopes scattered around the tennis courts like billiard balls on a vast table.

Dave Green checked his watch. He radioed Sir Amk Bittius IV.

"Mr. Green," said Bittius, his tone a symphony of false levity. "Hello, hello. We are still working to revive Yryssy Ayopy."

Toy helicopters *thitthitthit*ed; open-air jelsairs *osssh*ed through the air; Flok'embles *icawk-awk*ed as they hunted for bugs and small birds. Dave Green was oblivious to the noise; he heard only the crash of the waves of disappointment in his mind.

"I see. And are you optimistic?" said Dave.

"Oh yes," said Bittius. "Why don't you let me know where you are, so when Yryssy is awake, no time will be wasted?"

"I don't think so, Bittius. You just radio me when the

time is near. And that time had better be almost nigh or quite a bit of blood will be on your hands."

"But I—"

"Good-bye."

Dave Green clicked off.

CHAPTER 27

Chance and Braig found the golf cart in the theater precisely where it had been left. The machine started right up, and Chance took off down the hallway at top speed, Braig navigating from the passenger seat and screaming "*Emergency!*" as creatures of every conceivable form leaped out of their path. Eventually they rounded a corner and shuddered to a stop in front of 2222.001, through whose open door Chance was relieved to behold Mrs. Rurriery, who lay flat on her back on a gurney, an IV line leading from a vein in one arm to a bag of ichor hanging from a hook on a pole.

"C'mon, Chance, let's move!"

Chance undid the string of belts he'd wrapped around his waist, hooked one end to the head of Mrs. Rurriery's gurney, rolled her out into the hallway, and tied the other end to the back of the golf cart. He started off slowly, then picked up speed until they were careening along the polished linoleum floor, Mrs. Rurriery in tow.

"Be careful taking corners!" shouted Braig. "Go right at the end of the hall!"

Chance slowly decelerated until they'd rounded the corner. Then he took off at top speed again. Soon they came to a bank of elevators, one of which went to the 2,250th floor and beyond.

"We'll have to ditch the cart," said Braig.

They unhooked the gurney, with Chance re-wrapping the belt-rope around his waist.

When the elevator came, they wheeled Mrs. Rurriery, still serenely insensate, inside the crowded car and waited while it stopped at every single floor all the way down to 2,250, where the three of them disembarked. They made their way toward Yryssy's room. On the way, they stopped at a supply closet. Braig emerged with a yard's length of clear tubing, some white medical tape, and several cannulas, then they made their way as quickly as possible to 2250.984, which they discovered happened to be guarded by two outsize Balliopes who looked like they ate nails and drank lye and brooked no shenanigans.

"Hello," said Braig, carefully approaching the less menacing of the two. "We're here to see Miss Yryssy Ayopy."

"No entry," it said. "Begone!"

Braig and Chance retreated. Chance noticed that 2250.986, right next door, was vacant.

The Balliopes didn't notice when the trio ducked into the empty adjoining room.

"There's no way we can get into Yryssy's room," said Braig, wheeling Mrs. Rurriery into a far corner.

"But there is," said Chance. "We'll need a really long piece of ichor tubing, though. Can you get that?"

Braig ran out the door, closing it behind him.

Chance studied the room until Braig returned with twenty yards of clear plastic tubing.

"Now what?" said Braig.

"Climb onto the gurney," said Chance. "Straddle Mrs. Rurriery and stand up."

Braig did as he was told. Then Chance climbed on, praying the gurney wouldn't collapse under the weight of all three of them. He put the tape and the cannulas in his pocket and shouldered the coil of tubing.

"Now, hoist me up."

Braig laced his fingers together, and Chance put his foot in the stirrup made by Braig's hand.

"Now. One, two, three . . . up!"

Braig lifted Chance up to the ceiling. Chance knocked out the air vent grille and hoisted himself up into the

cooling duct. Once inside, he uncoiled one end of the tubing, attached a cannula, and lowered it down to Braig.

"Hurry," whispered Braig, taking the tube and sticking the sharp port cannula into the stent in Mrs. Rurriery's vein. "We have to do this before Mrs. Rurriery has metabolized all the flerk in her system."

Chance crawled through the air duct, letting out a little tubing as he went, until he arrived at a vent directly over Yryssy Ayopy's bed in the next room. He peeked through the slits. She looked an awful lot like Mrs. Rurriery. Emerging from one arm was a long tube leading to a bag of oily brownish-green fluid hanging from a hook attached to a pole.

And there a Deviklopt sat in a large chair, looking much like a younger version of Simon Sleight. It was dozing, its horrible, carious mouth wide open and drooling on its smock.

Chance lifted out the air vent grille. He quietly unwrapped the belts from his waist. The buckle on the end of one featured a small metal hook. Chance slowly lowered it like a hook on a fishing line into Yryssy's room. Reaching as far as he could, he guided it toward the long tube leading from the gross bag of fluid to her arm.

Yryssy's color had turned from a light gray to an angry, bruised slate green in just the few moments Chance had been here. She was dying.

He snared the tube with the hook and gently reeled it in. When it was within reach, he grabbed it and pulled it inside the air duct. Then he bit right through the plastic, pinching

both ends closed, keeping the fluid in the tube. He taped the end of the tube that was attached to Yryssy's bag to the cool metal wall of the air vent—if he let it drop, ichor would leak out all over the floor. He picked up the end of the tube stuck in Mrs. Rurriery's arm, sucked out the air, taped the ends of the two tubes together, and allowed the Geckasofts' ichor streams to mingle. Chance had no idea how long that would take, or if it would even work at all. Braig had said flerk metabolizes slowly, and that there might be enough left in Mrs. Rurriery's veins to at least awaken Yryssy for a few moments—long enough, perhaps, to allow her to tell them how to concoct and deliver her anti-GIGI drug, Ypocrasyne, to Dave Green.

Why wouldn't she wake up? The Deviklopt in the chair snored away.

Suddenly, Yryssy turned her head to the left. Then to the right. Her eyes fluttered open.

"What's happening here?" she said, croaky and creaky from her speechless comatose days. "Where am I?"

The Deviklopt in the chair bolted awake. Chance ducked back into the air duct and quickly put the grille back in place, leaving it ajar an inch so it wouldn't pinch the tube.

"Miss Ayopy," said the Deviklopt, jumping up from the chair. "It is I, Sir Amk Bittius the Fourth, chairman. I can't believe you're . . . never mind, I'm so thankful you're back with us again."

Chance watched and listened through the slits in the grille as Bittius informed Yryssy of the situation and then radioed Dave Green.

"Mr. Green, I've got Yryssy. Mr. Green, are you there? Mr. Green?"

"I'm here," said Dave Green, sounding existentially tired. "She's awake? Put her on."

"This is Yryssy Ayopy," she said, accepting the radio from Bittius. "You must come to room 2250.984, now."

"I . . . I can barely . . ."

"What? What?"

". . . move."

"Where are you, Mr. Green?"

"Middle . . . space. Floor . . ."

"Floor what?"

"I'm not—"

And the radio went dead.

"Let's go," said Bittius, lifting Yryssy into a wheelchair with the help of the Balliopes. "Wait. What is this?" He looked at the tube leading from her arm into the ceiling.

"No idea, boss," said the two Balliopes, looking at each other sheepishly.

"We'll worry about it later," said Bittius, pulling the needle out of her arm. "Now, come."

Then they were gone.

Chance allowed himself to think, just for an instant, that

all would be well, even though they still didn't know where Dave Green was. Chance backed up through the air duct until he reached the air vent he'd first entered. He looked down.

Both Braig and Mrs. Rurriery were gone. What the . . . ?

Chance let himself drop to the floor. He dashed out into the hallway. No Braig, and no gurney in sight.

CHAPTER 28

Pauline looked into the huge space with incredulity and awe. Of all the things she'd experienced in Saint Philomene's Infirmary for Magical Creatures—the harrowing mail room, the nine-mile elevator-shaft plummeting, the basement gloom, Rod Nthn's bone-and-bottle-cap throne—only the immensity of the serene space open before her gave her an understanding and appreciation of the true scope of the infirmary, and of the magnitude of potential destruction Dave Green held in one hand.

She needed to find him. Now.

She located a coin-operated telescope mounted on a

balcony nearby, inserted a blue-black clahd penny, and began to search the huge "sky," sparsely occupied as it was by balloons and other aircraft, until the rather fuzzy lenses began to give her a headache.

She turned the telescope over to an impatient creature waiting its turn. Pauline looked down into the depths. A few stories below her was a place that rented out strange teacup-shaped aircraft. She found a staircase that led to that floor. She waited in line behind a Vyrndeet dressed in a leather suit emblazoned with stickers and patches, like a race-car driver's outfit.

The rental agent was a particularly hideous Harrow-Teaguer with only one arm. It was giving the Vyrndeet instructions.

"Just drive it like a golf cart, except raise or lower the steering wheel to go up or down. Here's the throttle, and there's the brake. If you let go of all the controls, the craft will stop and hover. And remember, just press that big red button on the dash if you have any trouble, and the jelsair will automatically fly you to the nearest dock. And don't worry about crashing into anything—jelsairs can sense obstacles and will automatically fly around them or, if you're on your way to crashing into the ground or the balconies, it will simply stop and hover. It's foolproof. There's a telephone in there; just dial five-five-five, eight-two-eight, seven-seven-seven-seven to reach an agent if you have questions. Air time is five clahd per minute or a hundred clahd for thirty minutes. Just feed the coins into that slot by the eight-track player. If you run out of time and money, the machine will simply fly itself back here."

Pauline searched her front pocket and pulled out her cache of coins. She counted 155 clahd, enough for forty-one minutes in the air.

The Vyrndeet flew away. The Harrow-Teaguer guided Pauline to a jelsair and helped her step in. It was about the size of a small playground merry-go-round, and the inside, nearly six feet across, with seating for four, was shaped like a shallow cup. The single wing, like a ring of Saturn, was glass-clear. She put the top down, sat in the driver's seat, and buckled herself in.

"Have any ghouls rented a jelsair from you?" she said, on the off chance.

"Not lately," said the Harrow-Teaguer.

"Humans?"

"Serious?"

"Just kidding. Ha-ha-ha!"

"You're pretty funny, for a vampiress."

"I get it from my mother."

The Harrow-Teaguer put the top up, and pushed the craft away from the dock with one foot. And Pauline was airborne.

It took a few moments to get used to steering, but before long she was racing through space, flying as close to balloons and other jelsairs as she dared, looking for ghouls or humans.

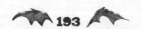

She had started looking for Dave Green around the 2,250th floor, but Middlespace was so large that she was able to cover only a minuscule portion of it. She checked the clock on the dash—only thirty-two minutes left. *There must be a way to narrow down the search!*

As she flew, she noticed that the fire jets used to heat the air in the medium-sized and large balloons roared like dragons, but the jets on the small armchair balloons for one made little sound at all. She thought about the sounds on the tape and the *osssh* of the jelsairs, the *icawk-awk* of the big pterodactyl-like birds, the *thitthitthit* of the toy helicopters. There had been no dragon-roaring on the recordings.

She concluded Dave Green could only be in one of the little balloons.

There were hundreds. Some were near the 2,250th floor.

Pauline flew from armchair to armchair, some many hundreds of yards away from the others, some floating in the dead center, others so close to the balconies that they were in danger of bumping into them. In one armchair, a Fauxgre near the north end of 2,277 had managed to get its balloon to spin in place; in another, an ouphe was flying a small remote-control jet in circles around his balloon near the center of the 2,315th floor, and in yet another, a teenage Wreau was deeply asleep in his chair, floating aimlessly near the 2,040th floor, high above her.

But no sick-looking ghouls or humans.

Only seventeen minutes left.

Then, hovering near the west end between the 2,270th and 2,280th floors, Pauline spotted a matte black armchair balloon. She accelerated the trusty jelsair and headed straight for it.

Pauline looked up and noticed all at once that somehow the ceiling of Middlespace had become . . . *blurry.* She rubbed her eyes, shook her head, and looked again. No, not blurry; there was simply a mist of some kind forming up there. A white mist that roiled and eddied and bulged. In a span of mere seconds, the mist congealed into clouds. They expanded until they became a bank of grayish-white cumuli blocking out the ceiling. Pauline was getting closer to the balloon.

Then the clouds grew darker. A half-mile-long bolt of greenish-blue lightning zigzagged through Middlespace, striking something far below Pauline and exploding in a fiery orange bloom, the sound of which reached her ears at the same instant that she heard the sharp-edged clangor of the lightning strike's attendant thunder. Pauline looked around her. Jelsairs and balloons and flying toys were all beginning to migrate toward the balconies to get out of the coming storm, but the balloon she was heading toward stayed put. And the fearless Flok'embles, who seemed to relish the weather, sailed about as always.

A great wind gusted, blowing Pauline off course. She adjusted just as raindrops started to fall. She was only a hundred yards away from the balloon. Then eighty. The rain was falling in sheets now, pitchforks of lightning stabbing the air all around her. Now fifty yards. It was when she was only thirty yards away from the balloon that she realized it was not occupied by a Wreau or a Thropinese, but by a ghoul. No—correction, a *human* with ghoulish makeup streaming down his face. His head lolled to one side. He held a radio in one hand, and his other was tightly closed around something. Pauline was pretty sure what that something was.

Pauline put the top down, exposing herself to the storm. She hovered twenty feet directly below Dave Green in case he dropped the vial, though if he did, she thought the wind would probably whisk it out of her reach. She couldn't stay here, she knew. She had to alert Chance and Braig and, ultimately, Yryssy Ayopy to Dave Green's whereabouts. Yryssy would certainly need to come to him because he appeared too sick to even get himself out of the storm. She hoped feverishly that Braig's plan, whatever it was, had worked.

Pauline was soaked. Water was accumulating on the floor of the jelsair. But she couldn't put the top up, because that would destroy any chance at all of her catching the vial should the "ghoul" above her drop it.

Then Pauline remembered something.

She picked up the jelsair phone and dialed zero.

"Directory assistance."

"Uh, would you connect me to—"

"Not *you* again."

"I know, sorry, would you connect me to Rod Nthn, a Thropinese? He's on the 5,999th floor."

"Please hold."

Pauline prayed he wasn't still manacled to his throne.

"Hello?"

"Rod?" shouted Pauline over the din of the storm. "It's me, your betrothed."

"Pauline, my dear, how I love you so. Where are you?"

"I need you to do something for me. To prove your undying love."

"Anything."

"I remember you said you could get on the PA and make announcements anytime you wanted to."

"Yes."

"I want you to announce something. Get a pencil and paper."

"Okay, ready."

"Announce this: 'Mr. Green, Middlespace, black balloon, west end of 2,277, Emergency.' Do it now, and repeat it once in five minutes."

"When will you be home, my sweet?"

"I'll be on my way the minute you've made the announcements. You're sure everyone in the infirmary will hear it?"

"Everyone."

Pauline hung up. There were eleven minutes left. Then ten. Then nine. The storm still raged. Why was Rod taking so long?

The PA crackled on. Though she recognized the voice as Rod Nthn's, she couldn't make out a word due to the

incessant storm. Good; neither would Dave Green. Then Rod repeated the announcement. Good ol' Rod. Maybe he wasn't such a bad guy after all.

Three minutes. Pauline scanned the west-end balconies, looking for Chance or Braig. She glanced up at Dave Green, whose one closed fist hung over the armrest, twenty feet above. He seemed delirious and didn't appear to notice the vampiress-driven craft hovering beneath him.

The jelsair abruptly began to move on its own. Pauline glanced at the clock. Her time had just run out. And there were no more clahd. The craft automatically delivered her to the nearest dock, a rickety wooden contrivance at the west end of Middlespace. When she arrived, she looked back at Dave Green in the distance, about two hundred yards away. As she docked, she noticed something far down the balcony.

Peeking out of the doorway to a stairwell in the middle distance was a slight fellow with a bandage on his head and bright blue ears some might say stuck out just a little bit too far.

CHAPTER 29

Chance was jogging up and down the halls of the 2,250th floor, looking for Braig, when a voice like a honking cat came on the PA system and announced that a certain Mr. Green was at the west end of Middlespace, whatever that was, around floor 2,277.

"They found him," Chance said to himself, turning down a long hallway on the 2,250th floor, now looking for someone, anyone, that he could ask where Middlespace was and how to get to the 2,277th floor. But there was no one to ask. *Wait, what's that in the distance?*

He could make out four figures way down the hall: two

Balliopes; a vast, scaly beast dressed in a dirty white apron with a blue-and-yellow horn emerging from its forehead; and a struggling Wreau trapped in a tall, narrow cage on wheels being dragged down the hallway toward Chance. He started to run toward it. Just as he got close enough to recognize Braig in the cage, the vast creature of uncertain make, who was apparently in charge, said to the Balliopes:

"Present . . . arms!"

And the Balliopes lowered their halberds to prevent Chance from approaching farther.

"Braig," shouted Chance. "What happened?"

"I got arrested for—"

"No speaking to the prisoner, Euvyd," said the vast creature, who appeared to be covered in scales that looked like the black keys on a piano. Each massive, muscular arm terminated in a hand consisting of two clawlike phalanges.

"Shut up, M'Quiminy," said Braig, who then turned to Chance. "Mr. Bee, they got me for kidnapping Mrs. Rurriery."

"You let him go," Chance shouted at M'Quiminy, but the chief of surgery ignored him, instead ordering the Balliopes to proceed down the hall, go left, and stop at elevator bank 1,004.

"Braig," said Chance, "are you going to the basement?"

"No, thank Saint Philomene," said Braig. "A special holding cell on the sixteenth floor."

"Perhaps you'd like to join him, Euvyd?" said M'Quiminy, smiling grotesquely, revealing sharp brown teeth that reminded Chance of broken oars. "No? Then shut your pink Euvyd mouth and scurry away to your ice-eared brethren."

"Chance," said Braig. "What about our patient?"

"She's awake. On her way. Braig, how do I get to Middlespace, floor 2,277?"

"I heard the PA announcement, too. Go back the way you came, take elevator bank 814 to 2,270, get off, turn left, go to the very end of the hall, take seven flights of stairs, and open the black door. Prepare to be shocked by what you see."

"Silence!" shouted M'Quiminy.

But Chance was already running back the way he had come.

When he finally reached the black door, he paused for a moment, then put one blue ear to the sturdy steel of the door. It sounded like there was a TV set on the other side, tuned to a show featuring a thunderstorm. Knowing Saint Philomene's, Chance figured there was probably more to it than that. He opened the door.

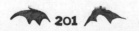

It wasn't a TV. Chance had never seen—never *imagined*—an indoor space with the dimensions of what was now before him. And he had certainly never imagined an indoor electrical storm. Drops of rain peppered his face. A majestic bolt of lightning struck a balcony directly across from him, on the other side of Middlespace, followed by a roll of thunder less than two seconds after. Knowing that sound travels a little more than a mile in five seconds, he estimated the distance between himself and the opposite side to be about a third of a mile. He ducked back inside the door.

He had not traveled to a gargantuan supernatural hospital to get struck by underground lightning. He closed his eyes, hoping for guidance from his father, but his father remained silent. It didn't matter; Chance knew that he might be needed, so he had to go out there.

Or maybe not. It was all out of his hands at this point, wasn't it? Bittius was in charge of getting Yryssy Ayopy to Dave Green. It was now just a matter of finding his sister and getting the heck out of there.

Chance did not want to go out in that storm, to put it mildly. But he did take another peek. As he squinted against the buckshot rain smiting his face, he heard, above the roar of the storm, a familiar voice.

"Chance!" it shouted from somewhere. "I need you, now!"

He peeked around the door. There was Pauline, way down the balcony, soaked, waving her arms and jumping up and down next to a wooden dock of some kind, next to which were a couple of teacup-shaped craft bobbing in the air.

"Come here!" she shouted. "Help!"

A bolt struck the lightning rod at the acme of a large red-and-white balloon moored to a balcony a hundred stories below. Chance was about to duck back behind the door, but he could no longer ignore the sound of his sister crying for help. He stepped out onto the balcony and ran as fast as he

could toward Pauline, the hair on his neck standing up like iron filings under a magnet.

"Chance," said Pauline when her brother arrived, already on his way to soaking wet. "Have you got any clahd?"

"Huh?"

She pointed to Dave Green and his balloon. "I have to go out there. In a jelsair. I need to hover under him, in case he drops the vial. And we need Donbaloh money to do it. I'm out."

"But Yryssy's on her way. Bittius is bringing her. Look, there they are now."

At another dock about a hundred yards down the balcony, Yryssy and Bittius were climbing into a jelsair, preparing to fly out to Dave Green, while a jelsair rental agent was gesturing in the negative at them, trying to persuade them that during a violent electrical storm was not the best time to go for a jaunt.

"Those things *fly*?" said Chance.

"Yep. Dave Green is close to death. He may drop the vial accidentally, or even break his word and drop it after he's cured."

"I don't have any clahd," said Chance. "Besides, you can't fly out there in this."

Then Pauline remembered. The mirror-shiny silver ten-clahd piece in her back pocket. It would buy her two precious minutes of flying time. She jumped into a jelsair as a bolt of lightning struck a balcony just a few floors directly

above them. Pauline was about to drop the coin in the slot when Chance said, "Wait."

He took a deep breath, innnn . . . ouuut, then ran out onto the dock and jumped into the jelsair with his sister, certain that a sizzling electrocution awaited them both.

Pauline streaked out to the balloon, stopping to hover beneath it just as Yryssy and Bittius arrived, their jelsair's wing just a few inches from Dave Green's right elbow.

"Sir!" shouted Bittius, as Yryssy unsteadily climbed onto the wing of the jelsair to get close to the man. "Mr. Green!"

Dave Green, all slumped in his armchair, moved his head the tiniest bit. He was not holding the vial so tightly now, and Pauline could see its lid peeking out from between his thumb and forefinger. Pauline hovered twenty feet directly beneath it. The falling rain felt like acid in her and her brother's eyes, the wind shouldered against them like linebackers, the lightning branched in irregular patterns all around them, and Yryssy Ayopy, anchored by a rope and balanced at the edge of the jelsair reached out and grabbed one of Dave Green's hands, the other, still holding the vial, too far to reach. Yryssy jammed a syringe filled with Ypocrasyne into the meat of his palm and quickly but cautiously withdrew to the cockpit to join Bittius.

Dave lifted his head up and opened his eyes. He looked around, still in a daze. With one hand he reached up to rub his eyes. The other hand, hanging over the armrest, opened like the great jaws of the infirmary mail-room iron claw, but instead of mail, it dropped a glass vial the size of a AA battery. It began to tumble in free fall, almost as if in slow motion, and Chance jumped out of the jelsair cockpit onto the wing and rapidly crawled to the edge. He reached out as far as he could, but the vial, caught by the wind, slipped by him less than an inch from his outstretched fingers and Chance slipped off the wing, barely grabbing the edge at the last instant. As he looked down at the wavering path of the vial, buffeted by the winds as it fell, the jelsair, of its own accord, began to slowly fly back toward the dock. Time had run out. He held on tight, the blood throbbing in his head, almost drowning out the screams of Pauline, who was trying to climb out onto the wing to save her brother, but the jelsair tilted alarmingly, forcing her back into the cockpit.

The vial was almost out of sight when it hit the top of a large celadon balloon, bounced high into the air, and was swallowed by a passing Flok'emble, who began to fly in large, lazy figure eights. Then it flew up, up, up in a tight helix until it was nearly level with Pauline and Chance, abruptly changed course, and headed in a path that would take it under their jelsair.

Chance shouted, "Meet me in the dressing room!" at his sister, and when the time was right, he let go of the edge of the jelsair's wing, falling through space until he landed on the back of the strange bird, Western style, and grabbed its long cars to keep from falling off. The Flok'emble was not

happy about this and began flying like a stunt plane through the dwindling storm, twisting, turning, diving, upside-downing, even rising up to the undercarriages of balloon baskets and jelsairs to try to scrape Chance off, but Chance hung on tight and the beast began to lose steam, now soaring instead of flying, dropping floor by floor, until the exhausted creature landed on the railing of a balcony some two hundred floors up, spectators running after them, some shouting, some clapping, others uttering appreciative sounds, and still others, whom he recognized as Balliopes, yelling, "Arrest him!"

The Flok'emble jumped down to the balcony floor, Chance holding on to the animal for dear life.

"Euvyd, it's illegal to fly Flok'embles," said the first Balliope to approach. "Let go of it and come with us. You are about to spend a night in jail."

"I order you to quarantine this animal," said Chance, with as much authority and force as he could muster. But the Balliopes, six of whom had now congregated, just laughed.

"Laugh away, Balliopes!" shouted Chance. "But I will make sure Sir Amk Bittius the Fourth knows it was *you* who disobeyed his direct order to put this creature in sealed medical quarantine. And you know what Bittius's rage is like. So I'm not letting go until you have this Flok'emble, who is a danger to every living thing in the infirmary, tethered and brought, personally, by *you*, to the nearest quarantine. Understood?"

Chance had never spoken with such conviction in his

life, and it must have worked, because the Balliopes muttered, "*Understood*" and led the animal away. They had forgotten to arrest Chance. The latest in a series of strokes of good fortune.

Chance was about to follow the Balliopes to make sure they did as he had ordered, but he was accosted by, of all things, a Euvyd, who blocked his path.

"Hey, buddy!" said the Euvyd, jumping up and down in excitement, keeping Chance from getting past. "That was amazing! I wish I had the nerve to do that. How did it feel? The wind in your hair and all? Looking down at certain death? Hey, what happened to you?"

The Euvyd poked at the soaked bandage on Chance's head. He had forgotten about it.

"Um, ow," said Chance. "Uh, I fell. Off of a, um, a Vyrndeet."

"Hey, what's up with your ears? They don't look right. This one looks like it's turning pink. Are you okay? Do you want an aspirin?"

"No, thanks," said Chance, backing up, realizing with horror that some of the blue makeup must have washed off in the rain. The Euvyd reached out and pinched Chance's ear.

"Ow!"

"Sorry, sorry." The Euvyd looked down at his thumb and forefinger. They were blue. "Wait a minute. You're not a Euvyd, you're a—"

Chance took off, trying every doorknob as he passed. The Euvyd ran after him, shouting, "Police! Police!"

A few of the ever-present Balliopes, aroused by the summons, picked up their halberds and began running in his direction. Two others materialized behind Chance. There was one more door to try before they caught him.

Locked. The lucky streak was over.

They were upon him. A lead-weighted net flew toward him.

Chance glanced over the edge of the balcony. Some ten floors directly below him, a purple-and-yellow-checkered balloon floated peacefully in the fresh, rain-washed air.

Chance climbed onto the balcony railing, took a deep yogic breath, and jumped as far into space as he could.

He landed just off-center on top of the soft balloon, bounced off at an angle and somersaulted in midair, heading right for a balcony, which he slapped into face-first, hard enough to loosen his teeth, but not so hard he couldn't get a grip on the railing. As halberds and nets fell past him from above, he climbed up and over, not a soul in sight. He tried the first door he came across, which opened onto a vacant stairwell on the 2,602nd floor.

Chance was glad he had memorized the name of Arbipift Obriirpt, M'Quiminy's personal bodyguard, who, as Chance had learned from the two Vyrndeets while he was hiding under the counter in the nurse's station so long before, might have the only map that showed humans how to get out of this place. But how to find Arbipift?

He needed a phone.

The best place to go was back to the dressing room. His sister had heard him, he was sure. They had to be together to escape together.

But could he climb 380 stories to 2,222? He had no desire to be on an elevator while his Euvydness was diminishing as quickly as his humanness was being revealed. So he had no choice. He bounded up the stairs three steps at a time, only occasionally passing a creature, none of whom even gave him a glance.

After forty stories, he was thoroughly out of breath. He stopped to sit.

Chance wondered if there had been enough flerk in the ad hoc infusion to cure Yryssy of Iptid's Misery or if she would succumb as Simon Sleight had. Chance wondered if Dave had been cured by Ypocrasyne and was on his way out of the infirmary. Probably not. Dropping the vial would rob him of his power over the populace, so he had probably been arrested and was on his way down to the basement.

On the other hand, Bittius might want to wash his hands of him and simply send him home. Chance thought this unlikely, as Dave Green would then have knowledge of Donbaloh that he might spread among the people of Oppabof, leading to lots of trouble for the infirmary, and the rest of Donbaloh.

Over the next several hours, Chance climbed another

thirty-five stories, slowly, stopping often to catch his breath. What was he thinking? He couldn't climb 380 stories.

He sat down in the stairwell, nearly defeated.

Then he heard a noise. A whiny buzz, like a weed eater. With some effort, Chance climbed up two more flights to reach the source of the noise.

There. A metal chair attached to a rail that ran along the baseboards, up the flight of stairs, and around the stairwell. It was a seat for the handicapped.

Chance sat down and punched the green UP arrow. The chair jolted into motion. It didn't move very fast, but it was sure and steady. It climbed one story in about twelve seconds, meaning that it would take a little more than an hour for the whole trip. He wanted to sleep along the way, for he was close to exhaustion, but he knew he needed to stay vigilant in case he encountered anyone on the stairs.

But he did not. This worried him. Maybe Terabug had been released and was killing everyone in the hospital at this very moment.

When he arrived, he peeked out into the hallway of 2,222. No creatures nearby. He stole out and located a room that happened to be occupied by two elderly creatures whose species Chance did not recognize, both hooked up to many machines and hanging plastic bags and sleeping soundly and noisily.

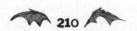

Chance closed the door quietly and tiptoed into the bathroom, where he put a foot up on the bathroom door's high knob, popped out a ceiling tile, and climbed into the narrow space that separated the drop ceiling from the floor above.

Around him was a universe of dust, dimly lit by the reflection of the light fixtures illuminating the floor below. Trusting his sense of direction, Chance began to crawl, taking care to stay on the narrow pathways to avoid falling through the flimsy ceiling tiles, hoping and praying he would come across the general area of the theater and its dressing room. His knees, still sore from crawling along the mail pipe—that seemed like so *long* before!—screamed at him.

After several hours, Chance noticed, far away, a square of light coming from below. He crawled toward it, wondering if he would have the strength to make it, because he was so close to holistic exhaustion. He finally reached the square of light, which was simply an air vent grille popped out of the ceiling of a bright room. He looked down. Three chairs had been stacked directly beneath him.

The theater.

With a scrap of strength he must have borrowed from some antimatter Chance, he climbed out of the ceiling and onto the chairs. He limped to the dressing room and opened the door.

CHAPTER 30

Pauline, her jelsair now automatically docked, watched through the last drops of the abating storm as Bittius, in the jelsair with Yryssy, hovered a few feet away from Dave Green's armchair balloon.

"Mr. Green?" said Yryssy. "All right?"

"My heavens," said Dave Green, rubbing his eyes. "What have I done?"

"Can you catch this?" said Bittius, leaning out of the jelsair with a coil of rope. "We're going to haul you to the balcony, all right?"

Dave caught the rope with some difficulty. They towed him to the safety of the balcony.

"Oh dear, where is my vial?" said Dave, staring at his bare hands.

"You dropped it," said Bittius. "A Flok'emble, now in quarantine, ate it."

"Oh. Well, it was empty."

"Empty?"

"I snatched it from a lab supply closet when I went on my rampage shortly after I got here."

"I see," said Yryssy and Bittius.

"Yes. I'm not feeling well. Are you going to kill me?"

"We are a hospital," said Yryssy. "We do not kill. We cure."

"Are you going to put me in jail like my grandmother?"

"We probably should, but no, we are not going to put you in jail. Your circumstances are extraordinary; you were not in your right mind, and we feel you cannot be held accountable for your actions. You are now cured, and your sanity restored. We are going to send you home."

"Oh. Good. I'm very homesick."

Pauline watched as Bittius, Yryssy, and Dave Green exited the balcony.

But Bittius poked his head back out, looked around, spotted Pauline, pointed at her, and screamed, "Arrest her!"

Pauline turned to run. She took two flights down, to 2,279, the floor she'd entered from, and kept running. As she passed the doors lining the balcony, she watched for red-lipstick Xs. In the distance, she heard whoops and howls. They were already on her.

Ah, here it is. She opened the door. At the elevator bank, she pressed DOWN and waited. Finally, it came.

Balliopes. Stuffed with them.

She grinned at them to show her fangs. They did not pay her much attention. Pauline climbed aboard.

"Where to?" said a very short Balliope with an extra-long halberd.

"Uh, 2,222, please."

She figured Chance would return to the dressing room in the absence of further information. It was a sanctuary, and there was a phone there, which they'd surely need to find Arbipift Obriirpt and get his map, which appeared to be the only way out. Pauline wondered if the map even existed.

The Balliope reached across the elevator with his weapon and pressed the appropriate button.

"Thank you."

"No sweat, lady."

"So, Chet," said another Balliope, "are we still hunting that Euvyd?"

The elevator began to ascend.

"Jeez, Dwilt, did you *sleep* through the meeting again?" said Chet. "Yeah, we're looking for the Euvyd."

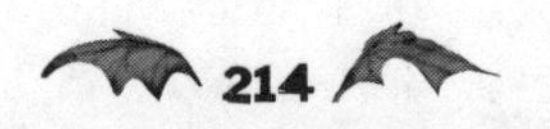

Pauline froze. She looked up, staring intently at an advertisement for a fingernail sharpener for fashion-conscious Vyrndeets.

"What'd it do?"

"I dunno. They just said it's wanted for interfering in official infirmary business."

The elevator stopped on 2,229.

The Balliopes bickered.

"Hey, why isn't the door opening?"

"We seem to be stuck."

The elevator suddenly dropped three stories. Pauline fell hard, smashing her head against the floor and knocking out her fangs. The lights went out. She was surrounded by darkness and flailing, wailing Balliopes. Pauline scrabbled around on the floor, feeling for her fangs. Pauline and the Balliopes eventually got to their feet and started banging on the doors. The Balliopes tried to pry them open with their halberds, but the blades were too thick.

"We're going to plummet all the way to the basement and die!" shouted an extra-panicked Balliope.

"Shut up, Bulp," said Chet. "This car doesn't even go to the basement. Just to 2,920."

This information did not appear to comfort the extra-panicked Balliope, who unfettered a cloudburst of bawling.

After several minutes, when it appeared no one was coming to rescue them anytime soon—their screams obviously did not register through two sets of thick double

doors, and the EMERGENCY buttons apparently didn't work—the Balliopes all lay down to rest. In minutes, they were fast asleep, their halberds standing in a corner. Pauline spent a few more moments searching for her fangs. But no, they were gone.

How to get out of here?

Pauline grabbed the extra-long halberd. She began poking at the ceiling.

There! A small door opened, the sort repair creatures might use to get at the wiring on the roof of the elevator. She hooked the halberd on a lip of metal, yanked on it to test it, and began to climb the halberd like a rope. When she got high enough, she grabbed the edge of the opening and hoisted herself onto the roof of the elevator car.

She looked around. In front of her were the doors to the 2,231st floor. She tried to pry them open with the halberd, but again the blade was too thick.

Pauline wondered how the doors knew when to open. *An elevator slows down until it's level with the target floor, then the doors open. Maybe the car itself trips a switch of some kind?* she thought. She looked up. And there, to the left, beside the door and just out of reach, was a small white button barely visible in the dark. She touched it with the halberd.

The doors slid open. She couldn't believe it. Pauline peeked around the corner. It was a dark floor, *thank ye gods*, and no creatures seemed to be around.

She stealthily slid inside, taking the long halberd with

her. It was only nine floors up to 2,222. *Careful, no mistakes now*—she was fangless. Once she was with her brother, they could plot their escape.

The dark, ominous floor seemed to promise a visit from the more dangerous and frightening Donbaloh creatures. Holding her halberd level, her back against the wall, she sidled along the wall until she found a set of emergency stairs. She climbed up to the brightly lit stairwell of the 2,222nd floor.

Set into the hallway door over the knob was a tall, narrow window with wire laced into the glass. She peered through it. She couldn't see any of her red Xs on the walls. The floor itself was teeming with creatures running, scurrying, skittering, moseying, driving golf carts, pushing wheelchairs and gurneys and laundry hampers and machines and towering carts loaded with trays of steaming unidentifiable foods. Pauline had not realized until now how hungry she was, how thirsty. How thoroughly exhausted.

A break in the traffic. Pauline looked both ways; there was no one around. She opened the door onto the hallway, barely noticing the smell of fresh paint, and sprinted in the direction she'd originally come from. But no Xs were visible anywhere. Had she gotten on the wrong elevator?

She noticed workmen up ahead, dozens of them, each doing something to a wall. One was reaching high above with a tool of some kind and another was on his knees doing something to a baseboard. She dared to get a bit closer.

They were painting. *Painting!* They had probably painted over her Xs long before. She was in deep trouble now. Pauline did not have the same infallible sense of direction Chance had.

Pauline passed a narrow door labeled simply POLE, and she was about to try its doorknob when an old, wrinkly Wreau wandered out. Pauline swiftly ducked into a nearby closet and pulled the door shut. She felt for a light switch but found none. She groped around on the shelves, which seemed to be filled with cloth of some kind.

Something touched her head. She ducked and uttered a squeak of fright, slapping at whatever it had been. She slowly stood up. It touched her head again. She reached up as quickly as a magician and grabbed it.

Hm. String. She pulled. Overhead, a light blazed on. Her heart felt like it was beating a thousand times a minute.

The room was filled with shelves of slate-green doctors' and nurses' scrubs in all sizes and cuts. Pauline set her halberd in a corner. She tried on a pair of bottoms. *Way too big. But wait, these will fit.* She eventually found a top. She found a cloth face mask, which she tied over her nose and mouth, and a cap, under which, with no little effort, she stuffed all of her wild red hair, still slightly damp from the storm.

There was no mirror, but she was almost entirely covered, and, with only her eyes showing, who would think a human was under all this?

She stepped out into the hallway. No one paid her any mind.

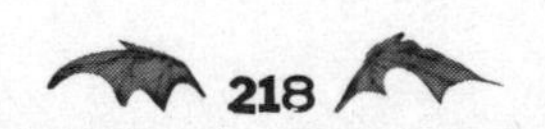

A commotion. Way down the hall. She stopped and watched as it came toward her. It was preceded by a clot of bumbling Balliopes, whom she recognized as the ones from the elevator, Chet in the lead.

Pauline also noticed two large creatures carrying a stretcher between them, upon which was what looked like a coffin. The creature in front was an especially silly-looking Vyrndeet dressed in yellow overalls, and the other was a particularly muscular Wreau wearing a paper crown. The procession slowly made its way toward Pauline. When it was within only a few yards, she realized the coffin was not a coffin, but a narrow cage.

Someone was inside.

Chance.

He was lying on his side in the cramped space, gritting his teeth and futilely trying to wrench the rusty but formidable-looking bars. Pauline leaned flat against the wall, and the Balliopes passed her by. Then she was walking alongside the cage, staring at her laboring brother, trying to get his attention, but he could not be distracted from trying to free himself.

"Balliopes!" cried Pauline.

CHAPTER 31

Chance, after his interminable crawl through the dark, dusty space between the 2,222nd and 2,221st floors, entered the sanctuary of the dressing room.

No Pauline, and, of course, no Braig. Chance sat down in a purple velvet easy chair near the telephone. He would have given anything for just an hour's sleep, but there was no time for that. Even though Dave Green was out of the picture, at least for the moment, he still didn't know where Pauline was. And Braig needed to be broken out of jail.

Chance stood up, picked up the seat cushion, took a deep breath, wrapped the cushion around his head, and screamed. And screamed. Then he practiced for a few moments, getting the voice just right. He put the cushion back on the chair, sat down, drew the little table with the telephone on it toward him, and picked up the receiver. He dialed zero.

"Directory assistance."

"Chief of Balliope security, please."

"Putting you through now."

"Police," said the being in the distinctive nasal chirp of an older Balliope. "Chief Fvendfvater here."

"Fvendfvater," said Chance, hoping the screaming had made his voice hoarse enough to convince the police chief of his identity. "This is Amk Bittius."

"Sir!" said Fvendfvater.

"Fvendfvater, there's been an error."

"Yes, sir. I will correct it, sir. What is it?"

"Indeed you will," said Chance, with the authority that comes from confidence. "On the—"

"Sir, have you got a cold?"

"Uh, yes," said Chance. "Now, on the sixteenth floor, a Wreau has been mistakenly imprison—"

"Sir, yes, sir, a misimprisoned Wreau."

"So you know who I mean."

"Sir, respectfully, that Wreau is a kidnapper."

"There is more to it than that, Fvendfvater. He was following my orders. He is to be set free and granted a full pardon, in writing."

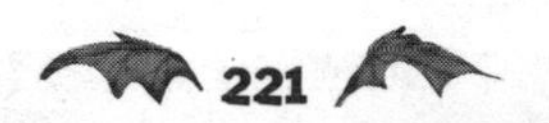

"Sir? The police don't issue pardons. You do."

"Uh, yes, I know that," said Chance, his confidence beginning to furl up. "I am hereby granting it."

"Sir, you don't sound like yourself. I'm going to have to ask you a security question."

"You doubt me, Balliope," shouted Chance. "Let the Wreau go free. Now!"

"Yes, sir, just answer my question. What was the name of your first pet?"

"I . . . I don't remember," said Chance. He foresaw doom and thick, rusting bars and death. "Now stop this nonsense and free the Wreau."

"Sir, who was the first girl you ever kissed?"

"How dare you, Balliope."

"Please answer."

"Er, I don't remember."

"Last question: Make and model of your first jelsair?"

"Um, Chevrolet Camaro?"

It sounded like Fvendfvater put his hand over the receiver. Chance heard his muffled voice saying, ". . . traced? 2222.560. Looks like it adjoins a theater. Get him. Now."

Chance hung up. He had to get out of there immediately. As fast as he could, he slathered his ears in more blue makeup and tied a new bandage over his forehead. He was about to turn and run when he realized that this might be his last chance to use a phone. He dialed directory assistance.

"Arbipift Obriirpt, Harrow-Teaguer. It's urgent."

"Placing the call now."

The phone rang. Chance listened for the chants and howls of the Balliopes, but he heard nothing. The phone continued to ring. And ring.

"Hello?" said a harsh, voluminous voice like Chance imagined Zeus might have sounded.

"Uh, Arbipift Obriirpt?"

"Who wants to know?"

"I was told you might have an old map showing how to get out of the infirmary to Oppabof. Do—"

"Where'd you hear that?"

"Uh, everyone says that."

"Izzat right."

Chance danced from foot to foot. *He had to get out of here!*

"Do you have it?"

"Can you pay?

"What does it cost?"

"If you have to ask, then you can't afford it."

"I'm just a poor Euvyd."

Silence on the other end of the line. Then:

"Come to 0013.550."

Chance ran to the door, but before he could reach for the doorknob, about fifty Balliopes barged in. They grabbed him with their twiggy arms, poked him with their sharp halberds, and kicked him with their tiny feet. Chance screamed and fought and twisted and rolled and bit and struck and kicked.

"We got you, didn't we, Euvyd?" said Chet, grinning monstrously at his quarry.

They placed him in a low, flat cage on a long stretcher and carried him out of the dressing room, through the theater, and into a long hallway. He yanked on and kicked at and tried to torque the bars, but they were too strong.

"Euvyd," said Chet, "you had the chief going there for a while."

"You've got the wrong guy."

Chance's line sounded corny even to him.

"Any idea of the seriousness of your crime?"

"I was just playing around."

"Not."

All the Balliopes laughed. They marched on. Chance worked at the bars.

"Balliopes!" said a voice.

It sounded highly familiar, but all Chance could see was some doctor walking alongside and staring at him. The doctor put a finger to the mask covering its mouth, implying *shh!*

"Balliopes," said the doctor, "what are you doing with my patient?"

Pauline!

"Your patient, doc," said Chet, "is under arrest for impersonating a figure of authority."

"And resisting arrest," added another.

"My patient," Pauline boomed, "was due in surgery ten minutes ago."

"He should've thought of that before he impersonated Sir Amk Bittius the Fourth."

Pauline couldn't wait to ask her brother what *that* was all about. She hoped she'd get that opportunity. She'd *better.* At that moment, though, things weren't looking all that rosy.

"Is that what you want?" said Pauline. "A corpse on your hands? Because that's what you're going to get if his surgery is delayed an instant longer."

The Balliopes stopped, as did the two creatures carrying Chance, and they all conferred among themselves.

"OR 2222.150," said Pauline, standing in front of the lead Balliope and gesturing to the left, at two swinging polished steel doors of an operating room. "Right here."

"But—"

"Now, gentlemen."

"We—"

"Let him out of the cage, and place him on the operating table faceup."

"If—"

"If something happens to him, I will make all of your puny, spherical lives infinitely more miserable than they already are."

"C'mon, guys," said Chet. "Bring him in. We'll just sit outside the door and wait. No big deal."

The Balliopes unlocked the cage and placed Chance on the table, then left—all except for a diminutive example of the species, who now stood inside the door.

Pauline dragged over a couple machines and a tray of instruments and green towels. She placed a clear plastic mask with a tube coming out of it over Chance's face, taped an IV to his arm without actually sticking the needle in a vein, lifted up his shirt to expose his stomach, then draped green sheets over him, leaving open only a square of tummy. She picked up a scalpel and looked back at the Balliope. He looked queasy. She turned back around, leaned over Chance, and whispered, "Okay?"

"Okay," Chance whispered back.

"Bear with me. Pretend you're under general anesthesia."

She removed the mask from his face.

"Chance," she whispered, "you were so brave to jump on that Flok'emble's back."

Chance was excellent at playing the anesthetized patient; he lay perfectly still.

After performing "surgery" on her brother for a good fifteen minutes, tossing "used" instruments noisily into the tray and plucking fresh ones out, dropping wadded-up towels smirched with iodine, which against the green cloth looked much like blood, Pauline looked over her shoulder. The sentinel Balliope had fainted. Pauline whispered to Chance, "Hold your breath and don't move."

Pauline ran out into the hallway.

"Balliopes," she shouted. "My patient is dead. This is all your fault, you kept him from surgery too long. I will have each and every one of your dense little heads brought to me on a surgical tray. Out of my sight!"

The Balliopes scattered. Pauline grabbed an unoccupied gurney and wheeled it into the operating room. Chance jumped on it, lay down, and Pauline placed a sheet over him, covering him from head to toe. She wheeled him into the hallway, whispering, "What now, Chance?"

"I know where Arbipift Obriirpt is," he said from under the sheet. "Thirteenth floor, room five fifty."

"Then that's the next stop," said Pauline, already watching for an elevator bank. "It'll be as close as we've come yet to getting out of here."

"But we also have to rescue Braig."

"What? Why?"

"He was arrested and imprisoned for kidnapping Mrs. Rurriery."

"Chance, we have to think of ourselves, now," whispered Pauline, jogging along. "We have to get out. The infirmary is okay now."

"We wouldn't have gotten anywhere without him," whispered Chance, dying to look out from under the sheet to see where they were. "It was Braig's idea to transfuse Mrs. Rurriery's flerky blood into Yryssy. And it worked. So we have to save him. He's on the sixteenth floor, in a special cell."

"If we're not careful," said Pauline, finally locating an

elevator that went all the way to the 12th floor, "all three of us will be in the basement wasting away, probably forever. We have to get out first, then somehow save him."

Pauline pressed the UP button.

"I can't let him down."

Chance was close to tears. He had never been more sincere, and Pauline could hear it in his voice.

"Let's talk about it when we've got the map. Maybe we'll figure something out between now and then."

The elevator came.

It was enormous. It could have held a small building. Or King Kong if he sat down cross-legged. But it was empty. Pauline wheeled Chance in. When the doors finally closed and they were alone, Pauline took the sheet off her brother and he climbed off the gurney.

"Good-*bye* and good *riddance* to 2,222," said Chance, reaching up to punch the button to the thirteenth floor.

"I'll say," said Pauline.

The elevator began to rise. Incredibly, it made the whole trip without stopping once. The doors opened.

The floor before them was a wide-open space three stories high, and apparently under construction. Creatures wearing overalls and lumberjack shirts wandered around carrying nail guns and saws and aluminum ladders and coils of copper hose; others manned big machines that jack-hammered, sliced, bent, drilled, welded, lifted, and crushed, while still others lazed around a watercooler, drinking something that looked like gray Gatorade from clear plastic cups. They stared at Chance and his sister with mild interest.

Lining the walls were thirty-foot-tall doors with big doorknobs in the middle and little doorknobs down at human height. Chance and Pauline began to jog along the first hallway. They were half out of breath when they finally reached 0013.550.

"I should go in by myself," whispered Chance. "Arbipift might get suspicious if there are two of us. He may not give the map to me, though—he asked me if I could pay and said that I couldn't afford it if I had to ask what it cost."

"Maybe we can trade something for it," said Pauline.

They both went through their pockets. Chance had nothing. Pauline had only a tiny flashlight, a couple AAA batteries, peppermints, and twenty bucks.

"Maybe this?" she said, giving her brother the banknote. "Can't hurt to try."

"Maybe he'll just give it to me," said Chance, his confidence in this possibility being roughly zero.

"I know you'll think of something, Chance. I'll be out here waiting. If you're gone for more than ten minutes, I'm coming in."

Chance knocked.

"Who is it!" shouted a deep voice from within that reminded Pauline of kettle drums.

"Uh, the Euvyd," said Chance, not feeling very brave.

"Enter."

With some effort, Chance turned the human-size doorknob, leaned hard into the vast door until it stood slightly ajar, and squeezed in.

It wasn't really a room. It was a cave. A cave ringed by huge glass-fronted refrigerators against every rocky wall. In the center sat a desk the size of a Dumpster. Behind it sat a creature, a colossus of the same species as Feargus M'Quiminy—a Harrow-Teaguer—wearing navy slacks, a short-sleeved white shirt with breast pockets, and a plaid tie. A stubby horn, glowing yellow and with a blue tip, stuck out of its forehead. Its hair was plastered to its scalp like greased seaweed, and its hairline dipped almost to its eyebrows. Its body was covered in scales that looked like the black keys on a piano, and its massive, muscular legs spread out on either side of his desk, which was piled high with papers and binders and in/out boxes, among which were scattered glass jars, each holding a semitransparent liquid, and some kind of . . . lump. Very organic-looking lumps.

"Hello, sir, I called about the ma—"

"Silence, Euvyd," it said. "Do you know who I am?"

"Uh—"

"Never mind," it said. "Come closer."

Chance hesitated. The room was perfectly silent. Well, almost; the only sound was a sporadic wet clicking. Chance

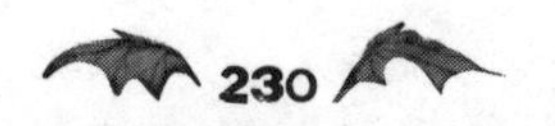

realized with horror that it was coming from the monster's sugar-cookie-sized eyes. He could *hear* the monster *blink*.

"Forgive my short-term memory problems," he said, "but didn't I tell you to come closer?"

Chance took a few ministeps forward.

"Now," said Arbipift, looking around his desk for something. "I know I have it here someplace. Ah."

Arbipift held a small, heavily wrinkled rectangle of dirty paper between his only two phalanges: a thumb and a forefinger, together large enough to encircle Chance's neck. He swallowed. The paper was limp from time and use, and it looked like a swatch of very supple leather.

Chance took another step forward.

"Thank you, sir—"

"Not so fast," the Harrow-Teaguer said, snatching the paper away and sticking it in a small floor safe. "That is a very rare document. In fact, I believe it is the only known copy. What happened to your head?"

"Oh," said Chance, reaching up for the bandage. "I, uh, bumped into a Wreau."

"Zat right," it said, leaning back in its chair and crossing its arms. "Is that why you're in Saint Philomene's?"

"Yessir."

"How come you can't leave by the regular channels?"

"Oh, uh, I can. I'm just getting the map for a friend."

"Who?"

"Oh, you wouldn't know her."

"Oh, a *girrrl*," it said, extruding the word from between his teeth like mud. "Say no more. That'll be twenty thousand clahd."

"I . . . will you take twenty Oppaboffian dollars?" said Chance, looking around the room desperately. "I'm just a poor—"

"Silence, again," it said with a low, heavy hiss. "Anything else?"

"Um, nothing."

"Why, I'll just give it to you then."

"Really?" Chance couldn't wait to tell his sister. They'd be out of there in no time!

"No, not really, sorry. But you *do* have something, er, *tradable*. You just don't know it."

The Harrow-Teaguer grinned. A thin line of drool fell from its lower lip onto its shirt.

"Wha—"

"Well," he said, settling back in his chair and putting his arms behind his head. "There's this little Euvyd girl, Pticia, down on the 4,816th, do you know her?"

"Uh, no," said Chance. Whatever it was Arbipift thought Chance had, Chance did not have. What did he want, his *clothes*? His galligaskins and Kippetore hair shirt and Möbius-strip T-shirt? If so, then Arbipift could have them, but that would kind of suck. Still, anything to get out of this place.

"Well. Pticia has some problems. Medical issues. The

most pressing is an unreliable kidney. One has already been removed, but you can't remove them both."

"I don't see how I can help," Chance said, but of course he could see.

"In exchange for the map," said the creature, "I'll be needing a kidney. Provided, of course, you are free of infection."

"Uh, I better be going now."

With the speed of a rattrap slamming shut, Arbipift reached out with his two phalanges, wrapped them around Chance's head, and lifted him off the ground. Chance couldn't see, hear, or breathe. He could taste the Harrow-Teaguer's skin, which reminded him of the time when he slid headfirst into home plate and got playground dirt in his mouth. Chance pounded on the huge beast's thumb.

Something was being wrapped around him. Around and around. Rope. Or tape. Once he was immobilized, Arbipift laid Chance down on the floor behind his desk.

"I will make the kidney decisions around here, ha-ha-ha!" he said while Chance gasped for breath. "I better tape your mouth up, too. Hold still."

"Waimmlph."

A knock at the door. From his vantage point, Chance could see under Arbipift's desk. The door opened. Pauline walked in.

"What do you want, trespasser?" shouted Arbipift.

"Oh, sorry, sorry," said Pauline, closing the door behind

her and touching her mask to be sure it was still in place. "Someone said you were looking for transplant surgeons?"

"*Who* said that?" the monster said, pounding on his desk, making everything on it jump.

"It's common knowledge," said Pauline, hoping her voice didn't betray the elevated state of fear that had seized her when under the door she had seen Chance's feet rise off the ground. Where was he now? He couldn't be far. After all, Arbipift, if she had heard right, was planning to steal a kidney from his body.

"I see," said Arbipift. "Well, you do realize some transplants require a measure of, er, discretion? Perhaps total discretion?"

"Yes, I understand. Anyway, hi, I'm Doctor, uh, Spock. I'm a freelancer, just offering my serv . . . Say, what's wrong with your eye?"

"Huh?"

"Your left eye. No, your other left. Yes. It looks milky. Mind if I take a look?"

"Um, sure."

"No, don't bother getting up. I'll climb up and stand on your desk."

"Do you need some help?"

"No, I can manage," said Pauline. She hoisted herself up. She stood and tiptoed toward the repulsive Harrow-Teaguer.

"Bend down so I can take a look."

Arbipift did.

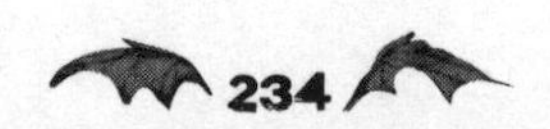

"Look up."

Arbipift did. That's when Pauline dropped something into the breast pocket of his shirt.

"Okay, look down."

"Am I gonna be okay, doc?"

Pauline glanced down behind his desk.

Chance. All tied up.

"Probably," said Pauline. "It seems that you have a case of, uh, halitosis piñatas. You should see a specialist. But there's no hurry."

"Oh. All right. Thanks. Now let's talk about a transplant project that's just come along. It's a little Euv—"

"Go, Mersey," shouted Pauline.

"Huh?" said Arbipift, jumping back.

" 'Oh, mercy,' I said. A poor little Euvyd."

The huge Harrow-Teaguer began to shake its head. Vigorously.

"What the heck?" it said, the tip of its horn turning from blue to red. Arbipift shook his head again, then held it between his hands, as if he were going to pop it.

"Get away!" Arbipift shouted.

He stood up, looking around desperately. Pauline jumped off the desk and ran around to Chance. Arbipift was now banging his head on the wall.

"Stop!" he shouted. "Stop! This voice in my head! Help! What do you want?"

He fell to his knees, holding his head in both hands

and banging it on the floor. Pauline worked frantically to remove the tape around Chance's head and body while Arbipift was busy with his agonies.

"Agh," said Arbipift, lying on his side in a fetal curl on the stone floor. "Anything, I'll do anything you say, just sto-o-o-op!"

"Get the map out of the safe, Harrow-Teaguer!" shouted Chance.

And Arbipift Obriirpt, Harrow-Teaguer invincible, got up onto his knees and crawled to his safe, dialed the combination, and removed the rectangle of dirty paper.

"Here, here!" he whispered. "Take it, you vicious sorcerers!"

Chance snatched it away, and the two Jeopards fled the room, pulling the immense door shut behind them, closing off the suffering Harrow-Teaguer for good.

CHAPTER 32

"W*hat*," said Chance as he and his sister ducked through a doorway, "was *that* all about?"

They found themselves in a library. An old library with sagging bookcases twenty feet high—books bound in brown or dirty white leather that were as large as seat cushions filled the lower shelves, smaller books were on the middle shelves, and the smallest sat up high. Ornate wooden rolling staircases circled every row of bookcases, at each end of which sat a huge book open on a podium—a dictionary?—that seemed to guard the library from vandals and desperadoes and all manner of the unwelcome.

It was dark as a tomb, lit only here and there by flickering gas lamps. Pauline and Chance were obviously in a little-used section of a vast athenaeum: the dust was a half-inch deep, most of the lamps were broken, and strange insects and spiderlike beasties crawled around, chasing and eating one another. Huge old wooden chairs were scattered about.

"I was watching under Arbipift's door," said Pauline, stepping gingerly between two rows of bookcases. "I saw a commotion. I 'called' Mersey and told her what was happening—that you were under the control of some monster. I told Mersey about the map and that I'd heard the beast say he wanted one of your kidneys in exchange. Mersey gave me an idea."

The books were so old that the titles had completely faded. Pauline pulled a book from the shelf. It was much lighter than she'd expected. It was written—not printed—in an unknown language, on thick, wavy paper, and in every margin on every page were notes in a tiny script. It reminded her of the note she'd traded back and forth with Mersey in class.

"Mersey suggested that I break the fulgurite in two and figure out a way to secrete half on Arbipift's person. Then Mersey would get in his head and torment him with Muzak until he gave us the map. And voilà."

Pauline held up the map. She directed Chance to pull up two chairs. They sat down under a lamp, placed the big volume across their knees, and spread out the map on its cover.

It was beautifully drawn and done in great detail. It was obviously old; no elevators were pictured, only staircases. There were no words, but the drawings suggested the twenty-fifth floor featured a door to a room that extended into the rock on the easternmost bounds of the infirmary. The door was marked with a skull and crossbones. Inside the room, in a far corner, was a trapdoor in the floor that led to a light-rail six miles in length, near the end of which was a five-hundred-step staircase that led to Oppabof. Where in Oppabof, it did not say.

"We're almost out of here, Chance," said Pauline.

"We just have to go free Braig," he said.

"Chance. There's no time for that. They'll be onto us before long."

"I'm going," said Chance, standing up. "It's only three floors away. I've got the map memorized. I'll meet you on Oppabof soon."

"But you don't know *where* on the sixteenth floor!"

"I'll find him."

"Every floor is the size of downtown Dallas!"

Chance hadn't thought of it like that.

"Still."

"Then I'm coming with you."

Chance was so relieved that he thought he would collapse.

"Good. C'mon!"

Just as they were replacing the ancient volume on the shelf, the door they had entered through burst open.

"There!" shouted half a dozen creatures: Vyrndeets, Balliopes, unknowns, all stumbling over one another. "Catch 'em! They're worth ten thousand clahd apiece, dead or alive!"

Chance and his sister took off between two endless rows of bookcases, heading for . . . what? They did not know. They *ran*.

They came upon a wall. No doors. But toward a corner, flanked on either side by a rusty iron chair, was a sliding glass door marked POLE, behind which was a tiny, brilliant-white antiseptic room, a complete contrast to the dusty, gloomy, cobwebby catacomb they were presently in; a juxtaposition of light and dark, old and new, clean and dirty. Only about the size of an ordinary shower stall, the room was empty except for three curious features: a hole about the size of a manhole in the ceiling, a similar hole in the floor, and, running centrally through both, a thick brass pipe.

The hoots and yowls of the pursuing mob were now modulated by the yodels of the ubiquitous Balliopes.

"What is that?" said Pauline.

"I think," said Chance, pulling the glass aside, "it's a firefighter's pole. Look, it says it goes all the way down to the 1,395th floor! Let's go!"

Pauline carefully stepped over a gap and hugged the smooth, polished pole, letting herself slide down, not too fast, not too slow. Twenty feet above her, Chance grasped the pole and started to slide, too. They stepped off at the sixteenth floor, finding themselves in a small booth.

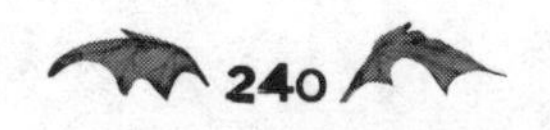

"What's the plan?"

"Simple. Watch."

The siblings opened the door and stepped onto a broad hallway lined with boring administrative offices. Creatures of all stripes, most wearing suits and hats and carrying briefcases, looking rather run-down, trudged up and down the hallway, glancing without interest at the Jeopards.

Chance spied an especially world-weary Wreau in a gray flannel suit pausing at a watercooler.

"Sir, can you tell me the visiting hours for the holding cells?"

"Er, by appointment. Just call ahead."

"Ah. And where exactly are the holding cells?"

The Wreau leaned over and examined Chance a little more closely. If it had any suspicions, it was far too tired and despairing to do anything about them.

"End of the hall, go right, left, right at the stuffed Flok'emble. Can't miss 'em."

The holding cells were simple barred doors, nothing fancy, each with a sleepy Balliope sitting in front of it. No sign of Chet.

Pauline and Chance suddenly charged the cells.

"Braig Toop!" shouted Pauline, startling the row of Balliopes. "Where is Braig Toop? I need Braig Toop immediately!"

Braig came to the bars of the second cell, mouth wide open, astonished. Chance put his finger to his lips.

"Who are you?" said the Balliope who appeared to be in charge, "and what do you want with my prisoner?"

"He is needed for an organ transplant immediately, Balliope," roared Pauline, "per orders of none other than Arbipift Obriirpt."

"Well, Arbipift Obriirpt can come get him himself."

"This is a time-sensitive matter, Balliope. Do you realize that Mr. Toop is the only creature in the infirmary with the kind of, er, flang bladder that is desperately needed by none other than a baby Balliope?"

"Really."

"Do you want the needless death of a poor, sweet, cute, helpless infant Balliope on your conscience?"

"Well . . ."

"And on top of it all, do you want to be tried for willful interference?"

"All right, all right," said the Balliope, fumbling with his keys. He let Braig out, and the three retreated in the direction Chance and Pauline had come from.

"That was marvelous," said Braig when they were safely out of earshot.

"You're going to have to stay in hiding until we can somehow get you an official pardon," said Chance. "I have an idea. Wait a few days, then contact Yryssy."

"I'll leave the infirmary for a while. Go stay with my friend Muge, out in the country caves."

"Good."

"Let's get back to the firefighter's pole," Pauline said. "We have to get to the twenty-fifth floor."

The friends all hugged. Chance and Pauline slid down the pole and got off at the twenty-fifth floor.

Just as he stepped off, Chance looked up and saw a tiny face ten floors above him. *Chet?*

Braig continued sliding down until he disappeared into the murk.

"They saw us," said Chance.

"It's okay. We'll work quickly."

They were in a large, clean, empty room floored in light green tile and furnished with what looked like the doors to minifridges, dozens of them, all protruding from a single giant steel refrigerator like windows in an Advent calendar.

In the rest of the room, tidy rows of gurneys stood in antiseptic silence. Most were empty. But one had something on it. A green sheet covered it completely.

"Oh dear," said Pauline, wrinkling up her nose. "A morgue."

"Do you think," said Chance, "there's any way *this* could be the skull-and-crossbones room?"

Pauline consulted the map.

"It sure could be," she said, folding the map back up and putting it in a back pocket. "Let's look in the corners for a trapdoor."

"I don't have to look," said Chance. "I can see from here there aren't any."

"What about under the big refrigerator, over to the left?"

"We could never move that thing."

The juggernaut of money-hungry citizens of Donbaloh who were anxious for a piece of the lucrative fugitive pie could be heard squeakily sliding down the firefighter's pole. *If only they hadn't seen us!* thought Chance and Pauline at once. *If only.*

"Hurry," said Pauline, "pile some gurneys up in front of the pole door. And the front door, too, for good measure."

The two Jeopards moved every gurney except the occupied one, piling them on top of one another, setting their brakes, until it would have been nigh impossible to get in without a battering ram.

"How are we going to move the cadaver fridge?" said Chance.

"Well, look," said Pauline, summoning Chance to the lower-left refrigerator door, a steel square with a handle. "Open it."

"You open it," said Chance, grimacing.

Pauline did. She pulled out the long, sliding drawer, which was, mercifully, corpseless.

"How in the world does that help us?" said Chance. "We still can't get under this thing."

Pauline pulled the smoothly sliding drawer out as far as it would go. Then she yanked, and the drawer popped off its rails and landed with a *thirk* on the floor of the morgue.

Pauline looked inside the hole where the drawer had been. She climbed in. She crawled to the very back.

"Hurry," shouted Chance, urgent, panicky. "They're at both doors. We're doomed!"

Pauline found a wooden trapdoor with an old, rusty iron handle bolted to it.

"They're getting through the doors," shouted Chance.

"Chance, get in and pull the refrigerator door closed behind you."

Chance did.

"Whoa, I can't believe you found it," said Chance, leaning down to pull on the trapdoor handle.

It was heavy. His sister helped. Finally, they got it open. Inside, it was as black as the Mariana Trench.

Pauline let herself down, holding on to the edge with her fingertips.

"I can't see the bottom. I don't know how far I'll fall."

"Just do it," said Chance. "They just broke into the room; I can hear them tearing the place apart looking for us. I'm coming right after you."

Pauline let go. She was in perfect free fall for a full second, then she hit hard rock, landing squarely on both feet.

"It's okay, it's not that far."

"Ow," said Chance, falling hard.

Pauline remembered her tiny flashlight. She switched it on.

They were in a great cave. The walls shone like mother-of-pearl, water shimmered in limpid pools, stalactites and stalagmites dropped and rose. In the distance, old railroad tracks glimmered.

"There's the rail. Let's go."

They jogged off into the dark, the little flashlight beam jumping with every movement. They arrived at an old but very ordinary-looking railroad.

"Just six miles. Careful not to trip on the ties."

After half an hour, Chance had to sit and rest. He had never gone this long without sleep.

"We've got to keep going, Chance. Can you stand up?"

Pauline took a step and suddenly bumped into something that knocked her back on her rear end. She reached out and felt the edge of a thin metal platform of some kind. On four wheels. She climbed on. There was a handle. Two handles on a crossbar, like a seesaw.

A draisine. A pump car.

"Chance, get up, I've found the answer to our prayers. Climb on."

Chance put all his weight on his end of the seesaw lever. The pump car started to move. An inch, a foot, a yard. It slowly picked up speed. They were now going five, ten, fifteen, twenty miles per hour . . . in total darkness. They would be there in minutes.

But where? How would they be able to see a five-hundred-step staircase?

Chance let up on his end of the lever. He was finally done. He curled up on the platform of the pump car and fell asleep. He had always been able to sleep in moving vehicles, no matter how shuddery or loud.

Pauline pressed on, but she was beginning to slow, too, exhausted herself.

Pauline realized all at once that she was able to see. Just barely, but there was something illuminating the way. There was no obvious source of light above her or ahead of her.

Ah. The minerals in the walls were ever-so-faintly glowing—enough for her to see her brother dozing on the pump car floor.

Way ahead of her, the cavern seemed to suddenly darken again, as if the minerals in the rock had decided for some reason to quit glowing. She closed in on the new darkness. Was this the end? Would she crash into a wall?

She squinted. It seemed like there was something up ahead. Or, more precisely, *nothing*. A vacancy. A vacuum. She squinted. The tracks ahead looked like they simply disappeared.

Then the vacancy ahead became clear.

A hole.

"Chance!" she said, grabbing her brother by the collar. He didn't move. She let go of the pump handle. With the same kind of strength that allows mothers to lift wrecked cars off their trapped children, Pauline picked her skinny little brother up and jumped off the pump car and onto the

berm, where they landed hard, both tumbling, the rocks tearing at their flesh and bumping their heads and bruising their bodies. The pump car hurtled on by itself.

Pauline slowly stood up and examined herself for injuries. Chance, wide awake now, gave himself a once-over. Lots of scrapes and cuts and knots, but nothing serious.

They walked up to the chasm into which the pump car had plummeted. Beyond it, the rail started up again. The hole was a terrific underground sinkhole that had probably claimed an awful lot of victims—pump cars, engines, entire trains. They'd probably abandoned work on the railroad a century or more ago.

Along one edge of the chasm was a narrow ledge just wide enough for a single human to shimmy by on.

"C'mon," said Pauline, not at all sure she was ready. But, of course, there was no choice. The staircase was certainly on the other side. "I'll go first."

Pauline inched her way onto the ledge. She hugged the dark rock of the cave wall.

"C'mon, Chance. You can do it."

Chance, refreshed from the nap and near-death experience, *knew* he could do it. He had practiced on a much narrower ledge in an elevator shaft not so long ago.

They made it to the other side.

And there, on the left, a recession in the wall of rock appeared. Set deep inside was an old iron door the size of a small movie screen.

"Look," said Chance. "The staircase?"

Pauline began working on the doorknob, which was rusty as a well-traveled anchor.

"Got it," said Pauline, unlatching the door and pushing it open.

Pauline reached down to give her brother a hand through the door. A vast, empty room revealed itself, its floor and walls made of huge stones intricately set in a diamond pattern. Moss and slickness covered everything, and insects scuttled at their feet. In the center of the room, a steep and towering spiral staircase of a reddish-gray stone flecked with gold rose like a medieval silo to the ceiling a hundred yards above, and beyond.

Each step was as tall as Chance's knee, each stair only a few inches deep, making for a very steep climb.

"Be strong, Chance," said Pauline, looking back at her brother and seeing utter fatigue in his eyes. "We're almost out of here. Think of being at home, seeing Mom, playing with Jiro. I'll give you my internet password and you can use my computer anytime you want."

"Really?"

"Sure."

With short rests every hundredth step, they eventually reached the 497th. Ahead, they could see a raised wooden boardwalk just wide enough for a single person, which was built over what appeared to be deep pools of clear, greenish water that led through a narrow cave. The cave turned a

quick corner, and a low, earthly light spilled from that direction. A faint mist, cool and refreshing on their faces, floated on the air: 498. 499.

500.

"We made it, Pauline."

Chance jumped around with the last of the energy in his benumbed legs. Pauline, all business, started marching down the boardwalk.

"C'mon, Chance. We're not out yet."

They picked up their pace, running along until they turned a corner and were stopped by something they had not expected to see.

A waterfall. Light shone through it.

"Look!"

The noise of the violent torrent was exceeded in magnitude only by the sheer volume of water that poured over them as they made their way through it. When they emerged from the two-foot-thick wall of water, they were in a clear, churning river. They swam to the bank, fell to the ground in utter exhaustion, and slept for six straight hours on the softest riverbank in all of Oppabof.

CHAPTER 33

It was early morning when the heat of the western Texas sun woke Pauline and Chance. Pauline dug in her pocket for the last fragment of fulgurite.

"Mersey!"

No answer.

Chance, sitting on the bank, looked up at his sister.

"Is this for real? Did we make it?"

"We made it, Chance. Well, kind of. We still have to get home."

The Jeopards looked around.

"Do you hear that?"

"What? The water?"

"No," said Chance. "Listen."

"A train?"

"I think so."

"I can't tell which direction it's coming from."

Chance stood up. He shielded his eyes and looked due south over a low edge of a canyon wall. He saw something strange.

Giraffes?

He was afraid to tell his sister that off in the distance he could see disembodied giraffe heads moving slowly eastward, four of them, hazy in the rising heat. She would think he'd lost his mind, and perhaps he had. But on the other hand, what bizarre things had they just encountered? What were a bunch of smeary giraffe heads compared to Vyrndeets and jelsairs? Besides, who cared what Pauline thought?

"Hey, sis, look. Giraffe heads."

Pauline turned, visored her eyes, stared into the distance. After a moment of analysis, she started running toward the low rise. She paused after a few yards, just long enough to turn and shout at Chance:

"C'mon!"

"What? Why!"

Chance was too tired to start running, but he did anyway. He followed his sister to the top of the caprock, where the siblings looked down upon something extraordinary:

The FanTan & Carlinda Circus train, moving slowly to the east.

"It'll go through Starling, Pauline! C'mon!"

And now it was Chance who had suddenly renewed energy. He took off toward the train, Pauline trailing by several paces. When they finally caught up with the seemingly endless string of coaches, it was moving so pokily they could easily keep up. They found an open boxcar and, with the utmost care, they climbed up and inside. It was filled with hay.

They watched the Texas landscape drift by, they waved at people in all the small towns they passed through, they dozed, they developed appetites, they started to recognize landmarks, and finally, when they realized they were at the city limits of Starling, Pauline fulgurited Mersey and told her to meet them behind the house in five minutes. And then, as the train passed the alley behind their home, Chance and Pauline leaped, one at a time, into the arms of Mersey Marsh. Door-to-door service! They all ran into the house, where they found Pye McAllister snoring deeply on the couch in front of the TV.

"Hi, Pye!" they said, startling the large fellow so badly he fell off the couch. "Just wanted to let you know we're home."

"Hrmph," said Pye. "How was your time at Mersey's?"

Pye did not look like he cared much how their time had been. He also did not react to Pauline's and Chance's appearances, covered as they were in scratches and bruises and cuts, five pounds lighter apiece, clothes dirty and torn, with Pauline barefoot and Chance dressed bizarrely and still sporting blue makeup on his ears.

"Pye, when does Mom come home?" said Chance, who had absolutely no idea what day it was or how long they'd been down there.

"Tomorrow, noon," he said, then climbed back onto the couch and went back to sleep; in minutes, he was snoring like a barge horn.

"I wonder how we're going to explain to Mom why we look this way," said Chance, who was scrubbing his ears at the kitchen sink, wishing he could tell his mother everything.

"Long baths," said Mersey. "And, Chance, I'll dab your scuffed-up areas with my makeup."

Chance wondered if he would be able to stand Mersey putting makeup on him. Just the thought made it feel like there were butterflies stage diving in his stomach.

Pauline grabbed her brother and Mersey by the hands and pulled them close to her.

"Our adventure has to be a secret. We can't risk someone hearing our story and believing it, then drilling a giant hole to the infirmary, or worse. So. Swear on your lives you will never say anything to anyone."

"Even Jiro?"

"Even Jiro."

"Even Mom?

"Especially Mom."

"Swear," said the three friends.

And with that, Mersey and Pauline went upstairs to her room and Chance to his, where he immediately fell asleep, dreamed of elevators, of fistfuls of shiny clahd, of legions of little round creatures, of the martyrs of lost causes, of the victims of injustice—

Chance bolted upright in bed. He ran to his sister's room and knocked on the door.

"It's me—Chance!"

"Better let him in this time," he heard Mersey say through the door. Pauline did.

"What is it, little brother? Want to kiss Mersey good night?"

Mersey puckered, and Chance turned so red in the face he thought his head must look like a bell pepper with hair.

"I need your computer," he squeaked.

"I don't—"

"You said!"

"Yeah, you're right," said Pauline, handing Chance the laptop. "Password's *gninthgil*."

And Chance sat right down on the floor while Mersey and Pauline crowded around him. He signed on, jumped on the internet, went to ChessKnight.com, and within a minute was a member.

"Simon and Yryssy used to hack into the Oppabof internet to play chess. Maybe, just maybe . . ."

Chance searched for *yryssy*, without luck. He tried *ayopy*. He tried them both backward; he tried anagrams; he tried *donbaloh*; he tried everything he and Mersey and Pauline could think of.

"She's not on here," said Chance. "I don't know what I'm going to do."

He put his face in his hands. He didn't care about anything anymore. The Balliopes would catch Braig, and he would go to the basement. Chance considered going back. After a good rest, he could load himself up with supplies, put together an unassailable disguise, and be back there in a couple of days by one of two routes. He could—

"Hey," said Pauline, "what was the name of Yryssy's medicine again?"

Chance, who was not optimistic because Yryssy probably knew thousands of medicines, searched for *Ypocrasyne*.

A hit:

The player is online, rating 2210. Would you like to play?

"Yes," typed Chance, not allowing himself to hope, for he knew he wouldn't be able to handle the disappointment if that hope were dashed.

A chessboard came into view. At the bottom of the screen was a dialogue box.

"Hello," typed Chance.

"Hello yourself," typed Ypocrasyne. "You can play white."

"Okay, thanks!"

Chance played 1. e4. Ypocrasyne answered with . . . c5, which provoked 2. Nf3, which Ypocrasyne countered with . . . d6.

"I'm Chance."

"I'm thankful to be alive," said Ypocrasyne.

3. d4, cxd4.

"Why?"

"Hard to explain."

4. Nxd4, Nf6.

"I'm lucky to be alive, too."

"Why?"

"I was on an adventure."

"Space travel? Skiing? Hot dog–eating? Visit to Hogwarts?"

5. Nc3, a6.

"That last one was pretty warm."

"Really? Where?"

"If I tell you, promise you won't end the game?"

6. Bg5.

"You're weird," typed Ypocrasyne. "Okay, promise."

"Underground."

Ypocrasyne paused for a full minute, then played . . . e6.

Chance played 7. f4. Ypocrasyne responded with . . . Be7.

"Where underground?"

"Donbaloh."

Again a pause. Chance played 8. Qf3, and Ypocrasyne immediately answered with Qc7.

"Just so you know," typed Chance, "I am not Dave Green."

"Who ARE you?" said Ypocrasyne as Chance castled on his queen's side for his 9th move.

"Chance Jeopard. I'm a human. A Wreau named Braig Toop is who cured you of Iptid's Misery."

"How did he cure me?"

"Flerk."

Ypocrasyne played Nbd7.

"Flerk," typed Ypocrasyne, "no longer exists."

10. Bd3, b5.

"It doesn't matter if you believe it. But Braig is the one who cured you."

"I must thank him. He is a hero."

11. Rhe1, Bb7.

Chance explained that Braig had been unjustly incarcerated to be tried for kidnapping, but had escaped and was on the lam.

12. Qg3, b4.

"If you really want to thank him," said Chance, "have Bittius give him a full pardon."

Chance played 13. Nd5, losing the knight in a sacrifice to Ypocrasyne's exd5.

"I don't know . . ."

Chance played 14. e5, beginning his attack.

"You and Braig, together, saved approximately 1,800,000 creatures."

. . . dxe5.

"Dave Green didn't really have a virus."

"But you didn't know that. Braig doesn't deserve to be in jail his whole life. He just wants to be an actor."

15. fxe5, Nh5.

"No offense, but how do I know all this is true?"

"Can you explain how you survived any other way?"

Chance played 16. e6.

"Did you mean to do that? said Ypocrasyne. "I'll win your queen."

"I meant to do it. Look, all you have to do is ask Braig for details. He'll confirm everything."

Ypocrasyne took Chance's queen, to which he responded by seizing her pawn at f7 for his seventeenth move, putting her king in check. She took the pawn with her king.

"I don't know . . ."

18. Rxe7, Kg8. 19. hxg3, Qxg3.

Chance told her about the transfusion from Mrs. Rurriery.

"All you'd have to do is go back to your hospital room and test the ichor in the tube in the ceiling for flerk. You can probably test for flerk, right?"

20. Ne6, Qe5.

"Yes."

21. Rf1, Nf8. 22. Bf5.

"Oh dear, that was a good move," said Ypocrasyne, defending with Bc8.

"Thank you," said Chance, proud of himself. It *had* been a good move. He followed up with 23. Rc8.

"You're still going to lose, though," said Ypocrasyne, playing Bb7.

Chance thought for a long time, then played 24. Bg6, an even better move. Then he said, "Your friend Simon Sleight gave his life to save you."

Ypocrasyne played Qf6, giving up her queen to 25. Bxf6.

"You know him, *too*?"

"I was in Donbaloh for quite a while. I saw you in the Middlespace storm injecting Ypocrasyne into Dave Green."

"I want to trust you," she said, playing gxf6.

"Check out my story. Then get back on ChessKnight and look for me."

26. Rxf6.

Yryssy said nothing. She took his rook with hers.

"Have Bittius pardon Braig."

And with 27. Bf7, Chance put Yryssy Ayopy in checkmate.

CHAPTER 34

Chance could not sleep. He checked the computer hourly for a note from Yryssy all through the night, but nothing came. Issuing a pardon probably wasn't the easiest thing to do in Donbaloh. At eight the next morning, Chance finally fell asleep, not waking until a commotion downstairs woke him at noon.

Chance jumped out of bed and checked the computer.

Yryssy!

"Chance," wrote Yryssy, forgoing chess altogether, "Bittius pardoned Braig. He even got a medal."

Chance leaped into the air and cheered, reawakening every injury to his person. "Ow!"

"And Dave Green," continued Yryssy, "is officially off the premises and safely back in Lubbock."

Chance thanked Yryssy, then gingerly dressed and went downstairs, where he found his mother, Mersey, and Pauline all sitting at the kitchen table playing hearts with Daisy's bridge cards and eating peach yogurt.

"There you are," said Daisy, getting up to give her son a peck on the forehead. "You're wearing long sleeves, too? It's such a hot day! You and your sister. Well, get a yogurt and sit down and tell us all about your adventures while I was away."

Chance, Pauline, and Mersey began to giggle, a bubbly chorus they tried and failed to suppress, and that simply redoubled the power of the original giggles, which soon turned to breathless laughter so infectious that Mrs. Daisy Bopp Jeopard could not help but join in.

After the quartet's last peal of mirth, the game of hearts resumed, though none of them really had much investment in it; each of them had much on their minds. Daisy was thinking her children had been up to something—something big—while she was gone, but she couldn't imagine what it was. It was almost as if they'd been abducted by curious aliens who ran them through batteries of tests before returning them to Earth. But something like that was, of course, ridiculous.

Still, they seemed more . . . self-possessed. Mature. *Able*. More than a mere week could account for.

Mersey Marsh was hoping Arbipift the Harrow-Teaguer hadn't found the fulgurite fragment in his shirt pocket, because she had been broadcasting a suite of yodels she downloaded from the internet in the hope of driving him bananas. It made Mersey furious to think of Arbipift and his plans to pinch a kidney from the only boy she knew who was genuinely courageous. Certainly more so than the coward Josh Ringle. Yesterday, when he had come knocking after a dramatic breakup with Clarissa Speen, Mersey had slammed the door right in his face. He was cute, but he had no character, and Mersey would no longer deal with characterless beauties.

Pauline Dearie Jeopard was thinking hard about the difference between bravery and courage, finally deciding that bravery was unmindful fearlessness acting for itself, while courage was being in a state of fear but acting in the face of it for the good of many. She was merely brave; her brother was courageous. She loved him for this, more than she ever had before.

When she had first emerged from the waterfall, Pauline vowed to forget all that had happened to them: the risks they'd taken, the nightmarish creatures and scenarios, the constantly hovering scythe of death poised to abbreviate them. But as time went on, Pauline came to tolerate, then like, and then treasure the memories.

Chance Bee Jeopard, instead of paying attention to the game of hearts, was in the process of swearing on his father's grave that he would never again dig a hole. And he would never access any portal whose terminus was unknown. Though Chance would never be able to shed his persona as a tester of limits, his acuity at gauging whether a limit should be tested at all had sharpened considerably, this process of honing having taken place miles underground in the very recent past.

Chance never told anyone about the infirmary, but he did write and draw an entire graphic novel that told a story not unlike his own. It was in the middle of the present game of hearts that he got the idea.

"Your turn, sibling," said Pauline.

Before he could play, an unheralded thunderclap and its flashbulb-bright flare of lightning startled them all.

"Just a minute," said Pauline, who placed her cards on the table and stood up.

"Hey, you're not going out there," said all her companions at once.

Pauline didn't answer. Instead, she went upstairs to her room, opened the drapes that covered the big picture window that looked west over the plains and big sky, and sat on a pillow on the floor to watch the huge thundercloud with its flagrant claws of lightning move quickly toward her. Between the crackles and roars of thunder, Pauline called to everyone downstairs and asked them to come up. She

arranged two chairs and another pillow alongside her own. When they arrived, they each took a spot, made themselves comfortable, and put aside their manifold fears, thoughts, and worries to witness the marvelous, potent, incomparable theater of an approaching Texas thunderstorm.

APPENDIX

CREATURES MENTIONED OR REFERRED TO IN THE TEXT

BALLIOPE: Donbalese. Short, spherical beast with long antennae and a taste for law and order. Common. Species forms the infantry of Saint Philomene's Infirmary for Magical Creature's security forces. Sleeps a lot.

BARROW-WIGHT: Oppaboffian. Tolkienian Middle-earth creature of great rarity, little seen at Saint Philomene's.

BLUTCH SPIDER: Donbalese. Endangered ten-legged pseudo-arachnid the size of a van that spins webs in the corners of large spaces, capturing birds and insects and the occasional Flok'emble. Can live for twenty-five years without food.

BRUX: Donbalese. Small creature that resembles a Shop-Vac in a fur coat. Prone to psychiatric illnesses. Archenemy of the Thropinese; special care is taken in Saint Philomene's to keep them separated.

DEMON: Oppaboffian and Donbalese. There are thousands of variants of this ill-natured pink or reddish humanoid designed to torment other creatures. Banned on certain floors and in Middlespace. Excellent IT skills. Usually admitted to Saint Philomene's for dermatological disorders.

DEVIKLOPT: Donbalese. Elfin creature notorious for its copious production of bodily oils. Highly intelligent, without street sense, and given to hifalutin babel, but loyal and selfless. Seems to suffer every known ailment.

EUVYD: Oppaboffian and Donbalese. Similar to the human in appearance, but biologically unrelated. Identifiable by bright blue, sticking-out ears, translucent hair, and black spider veins on the forehead. Gregarious and fearless. Commonly found working in libraries and bookstores. Were once the only link to Oppabof, where they labored as customs agents for imports and exports.

FAIRY: Oppaboffian. Diminutive humanoid that occurs in many varieties and forms, depending on its origin. Usually

winged. Widely seen in Saint Philomene's as both patient and resident. Such avid followers of the biannual World Cup that fairy gangs form and brawl, occasionally causing great damage.

FAIRY GODMOTHER: Oppaboffian. Humanoid mentor to humans and supernatural creatures alike. Examples in literature sometimes do not conform to the real McCoy, which is placid, non-confrontational, agoraphobic, and likes to solve sudoku and dispense advice to youths from time to time. Born old; no fairy godmother is known to be less than sixty-four.

FAUXGRE: Donbalese. An intimidating beast and ogre lookalike, the Fauxgre has little in common with the true ogre, save great strength; it is a serene, sleepy being of no minor mental limitation. Usually admitted to Saint Philomene's for severe hiccups and nosebleeds, though untreatable meteorism is often seen. Most of the species work as bookbinders, printers, or standup comedians.

FLOK'EMBLE: Donbalese. Endangered. Graceful, birdlike creature resembling a black hamster crossed with a pterodactyl. Lives alone, mating once in a lifetime. Almost all known examples thrive in Middlespace.

GECKASOFT: Donbalese. An intelligent creature not unlike the Oppaboffian film star E.T. in appearance, but delicate and slender. Known for intelligence, bad breath,

and an unfortunate biological magnetism to virtually any disease. Powerfully resourceful, it is sometimes the last resort for doctors confronted with otherwise incurable diseases, yet a Geckasoft cannot treat itself. Fine chess and Go player.

GHOUL: Oppaboffian. Related to the revenant and zombie, this quasi-human is usually found nosing around the morgue. Whitish pallor, shrunken lips, often admitted for gum disease. Antisocial, boring.

GIANT CPULBA: Donbalese. Lovable, roundish furry creature that travels by hopping. Susceptible to tricks and pranks. The teenage Cpulba tends toward shyness and nerdiness, but becomes sociable and cuddly when mature. Generally finds employment as an ocular surgeon.

HARROW-TEAGUER: Donbalese. Twenty-foot colossus covered in black wood-like scales, with arms ending in two powerful phalanges that can pinch a garbage can flat. Tidy dresser, has gambling issues, is superstitious. There are no females; a Harrow-Teaguer reproduces by chopping off the end of its tail and placing it in a dish of ice water.

HUMAN: Oppaboffian. Overprivileged species of shallow import. Carrier of disease. Warmonger. Invented the Reuben.

HURLWORM: Donbalese. Parasitic beast resembling a wedding ring that proliferates in the guts of unlucky

Tepesettes, who usually contract it by eating undercooked Brux.

KALLASP: Donbalese. Inextinguishable menace to all beings in Donbaloh. Large spherical insect, half of whose body is a sac filled with a concentrated hemotoxin that it likes to inject into any beast larger than itself. Impervious to poisons, impossible to catch, and without natural enemies.

KELPIE: Oppaboffian. Horse-like marine creature capable of transforming into a humanoid bathing beauty to lure human children into the water so it can eat them. Generally healthy, kelpies seldom need the services of the Infirmary, except when they've consumed an indigestible child, in which case an emergency transfer from Oppabof must be actioned.

KRAKEN: Oppaboffian. Vast, squid-like sea monsters. One of the very few creatures to whom the Infirmary is obliged to send a team of doctors to treat it, usually to remove barnacles. A kraken seldom pays its hospital bill, and collection efforts often fail.

LESSER PERDELIDS: Donbalese. Graceful, playful winged creature resembling a dove crossed with a paper airplane. Lives exclusively in Middlespace. Once used as a messenger. Greater Perdelids are long extinct; there are two Middling Perdelids in captivity, but they refuse to mate.

LOYOY: Donbalese. A duck-like creature cultivated for food on the Infirmary's farm floors. When properly prepared, a superior delicacy; when overcooked, a bit like a chew toy.

MANTLE RAT: Donbalese. An almost mythically hideous creature not unlike a miniature black bear with long, spidery legs. Scurries around the catacombs and the basement eating whatever it sees, including the outstretched limbs of sleeping prisoners. Well-dressed, reportedly telepathic, and lives to a great old age.

OGRE: Oppaboffian. Well-known creature-eating monster, very large, obliged to take special elevators and live on custom-built, dedicated wards. Smelly; malingering.

OUPHE: Oppaboffian. An elfin changeling forever suffering from treatment-resistant despair. Often volunteers to road test new psychiatric medicines. Excels at video games.

PIXIE: Oppaboffian. Archenemy of the fairy. Benign, likable beast often admitted to the Infirmary in groups of several hundred, all having come down with the same infirmity at the same time, usually botulism or lice.

POLTERGEIST: Oppaboffian. A noisy ghost, sometimes without form. Insufferable as a patient or employee ever since the species rose to fame in a 1982 film. Usually admitted for trifocal fittings.

QUERQUETULANA: Oppaboffian. Oak-grove tree nymph. Fleet and retiring. Rare. Often suffers from extreme homesickness while in the Infirmary.

REVENANT: Oppaboffian. Humanoid related to the zombie, but usually not so messed up. Occasionally seen in the Infirmary's catacombs and crawling between floors. Obstinate, at war with reason, but susceptible to hypnotic control.

SHELLYCOAT: Oppaboffian. Aquamarine bogeyman. Often admitted for severe water on the ear, hypothermia, the bends. Generally guileless and dim. Fine swimmer. Reputedly talented at parlor games, but has no social skills and is resistant to psychotherapy.

SOWLTH: Oppaboffian. Specter. Plagued by cataracts and poor night vision. Often has imaginary friends. Rare.

SUPERHERO: Oppaboffian. Class of beings, mostly humanoid, elevated to a higher plane of existence by virtue of superior intelligence, an extra power, sense, or ability. Often in costume, generally in startlingly good shape. Ailments are myriad. Frequently treated as celebrities while at Saint Philomene's.

TEPESETTE: Donbalese. Delicate creature with gastrointestinal issues and at high risk of brain fulse, a terminal

condition characterized by small cerebral mushrooms. Skilled at small talk, but cannot discuss deeper issues.

THROPINESE: Donbalese. Horrible creature not unlike a dog-sized beetle dressed for aerobics. Hyperactive mucosal glands. Flatterer. Rather simple. Females of the species are extremely rare; in desperation males will woo females of other species. Loves parties.

UNMAN: Donbalese. Magical creature resembling a mouse skeleton. Lives in symbosis with an Oppaboffian algae. Susceptible to kenicki-quithers, a fatal syndrome involving shrinkage of the hindquarters.

VAMPIRE: Oppaboffian. Very common humanoid bloodsucker. Lives a long time, but has a delicate subconscious, and is generally admitted to the Infirmary for long-term psychoanalysis. A troublemaker; sleepy.

VIZARD: Oppaboffian. An ordinary specter. Not seen in Donbaloh for half a millennium, though there is one pickled in formaldehyde in the Thousandth-Floor Museum.

VYRNDEET: Donbalese. Smelly, comically structured beast nearly ten feet tall. Employed in menial positions at the Infirmary. Suffers from chronic fatigue and sociopathy. Smells like low tide.

WEREWOLF: Oppaboffian. Nocturnal lupine-human

ravager of innocents. Generally not permitted in Donbaloh, but exceptions are made for the terminally ill.

WIZARD: Oppaboffian. Humanoid seer and magician. Not as immortal as it thinks it is. Usually admitted to the Infirmary for sleep disorders. Wizened, grouchy, and particularly dangerous on the squash court.

WREAU: Donbalese. Well-respected, five-foot-tall creature not unlike a shaved meerkat. An impeccable dresser, clever, and has a penchant for the stage. Particularly agile representatives of the species are often chosen as cheerleaders for various sporting contests. Long-lived, but an endangered species.

ZOMBIE: Oppaboffian. An animated human corpse, the only version of a human permitted in Donbaloh. Usually admitted for cosmetic surgery, though some are employed as baristas. Slow and ill-spoken. Often seen with its arms sticking out.

AN ACKNOWLEDGMENT

The moves in Chance and Ypocrasyne's chess match follow those in a game between Czech grandmaster David Navara (FIDE 2728) and master Jan Helbich Sr. (FIDE 2136) at the Energy Cup Tournament in 1998: 1. e4 c5 2. Nf3 d6 3. d4 cd4 4. Nd4 Nf6 5. Nc3 a6 6. Bg5 e6 7. f4 Be7 8. Qf3 Qc7 9. O-O-O Nbd7 10. Bd3 b5 11. Rhe1 Bb7 12. Qg3 b4 13. Nd5 ed5 14. e5 de5 15. fe5 Nh5 16. e6 Ng3 17. ef7 Kf7 18. Re7 Kg8 19. hg3 Qg3 20. Ne6 Qe5 21. Rf1 Nf8 22. Bf5 Bc8 23. Re8 Bb7 24. Bg6 Qf6 25. Bf6 gf6 26. Rf6 Re8 27. Bf7#

ACKNOWLEDGMENTS

I am deeply grateful for the support and cheerleading of the following people: Sam Anderson-Ramos, Rebecca Beegle, Wayne Alan Brenner, R. J. Casey, Marcio Coello, Pamela Colloff, Cathy Cotter, Bob Cotter, Albert Cotton, Betty Cotton, Karen Davidson, Kay Davis, Ron DeGroot, Brian Dempsey, Melissa Dempsey, Rob Duncan, Adam Eaglin, Joe Etherton, Karen Etherton, Jennifer Fahrenbacher, Billy Fatzinger, Pansy Flick, Elliott Flick, Laura Godwin, Nancy Gore, Gaylon Greer, Keith Harmon, Bill Hartman, Marilyn Hartman, Anna Margaret Hollyman, Helen Hollyman, Christine Horn, Ian Jackson, Jackie Kelly, Sara Kocek, Annie La Ganga, Maria La Ganga, Michael Laird, Robert Melton, Delaine Mueller, Stacy Muszynski, Carly Nelson, John Norris, Lenka Norris, Kim Kronzer O'Brien, Becka Oliver, Krissy Olson, Diane Owens, Mary Jo Pehl, Bryan Sansone, Julia Sooy, Marilyn Vaché, and REYoung.